NATURAL CONSEQUENCES

NATURAL CONSEQUENCES

ELIA BARCELÓ

TRANSLATED BY
Yolanda Molina-Gavilán & Andrea Bell

Vanderbilt University Press
Nashville, Tennessee

Library of Congress Cataloging-in-Publication Data

Names: Barceló, Elia, author. | Molina-Gavilán, Yolanda, translator. |
  Bell, Andrea L., 1960– translator.
Title: Natural consequences : a novel / Elia Barceló ; translated by
  Yolanda Molina-Gavilán and Andrea L. Bell.
Other titles: Consecuencias naturales. English
Description: Nashville, Tennessee : Vanderbilt University Press, [2021] |
  Includes bibliographical references. | Summary: "A feminist, gender
  swapping space farce from one of the world's masters of speculative
  fiction" – Provided by publisher.
Identifiers: LCCN 2021030602 (print) | LCCN 2021030603 (ebook) | ISBN
  9780826502339 (paperback) | ISBN 9780826502346 (epub) | ISBN
  9780826502353 (PDF)
Subjects: LCGFT: Novels.
Classification: LCC PQ6652.A6618 C613 2021 (print) | LCC PQ6652.A6618
  (ebook) | DDC 863/.64—dc23
LC record available at https://lccn.loc.gov/2021030602
LC ebook record available at https://lccn.loc.gov/2021030603

Cover design: Illustration adapted from the cover design by Alvin Lustig (1915–1955)
for Paul Bowles's *The Sheltering Sky* (New York: New Directions, 1949).

To Antonio, my beloved brother
Yolanda Molina-Gavilán

To my Hamline students, with gratitude
Andrea Bell

CONTENTS

ACKNOWLEDGMENTS

I would like to acknowledge the students who took my 2021 winter term SP407 Hispanic Women Writers course for reading *Natural Consequences* in the original Spanish and sharing their fresh perspectives about the novel with me. Also, my sincere thanks to Suzan Harrison, our Vice President for Academic Affairs and Dean of Faculty at Eckerd College, for her support of this project.

Yolanda Molina-Gavilán

I've dedicated this book to my students at Hamline University, past, present, and future, for they are what I value and love most about being a college professor. I'd also like to acknowledge one recent student, Nick Hill ('20, Spanish and legal studies), who collaborated with me on translating Chapter 5 of this novel. Nick was a pleasure to work with and brought many fresh ideas to the page. I hope the fatigue he sometimes felt from questioning every translation choice was offset by the glory of finding just the right word.

Andrea Bell

Our sincere thanks to our visionary editor at Vanderbilt University Press, Zachary Gresham, and to Joell Smith-Borne for reading our manuscript with a copyeditor's eye and a storyteller's heart.

YMG and ALB

INTRODUCTION

Natural Consequences and Its Author, Elia Barceló

Elia Barceló (1957–), a native of Elda, Alicante, Spain, spent most of her career as a professor of literature at the University of Innsbruck, Austria. She has worked as a full-time writer since 2017. Barceló is undoubtedly one of the most relevant Spanish science fiction authors of her generation and was recognized as such in 2007 when she was awarded the Gabriel Prize for a lifetime's achievement in the genre. Her oeuvre, not all of it written within the parameters of science fiction, has been translated into several languages and includes twenty-seven books and more than sixty short stories. In a recent interview, Barceló revealed that her interest in speculative fiction began as a child, when she first discovered the power of the genre to fill her with wonder and open her mind to endless possibilities. It can also revitalize literature itself. In the same interview, Barceló gives a clue as to the eclecticism of her literary production by explaining that her writing process doesn't begin by thinking in terms of genre,

---

Please note this introduction contains minor plot spoilers.

but rather by falling in love with a story first (Heredia 2014). Barceló's literary production, often directed toward a young adult audience, almost never strays from the extraordinary mode of literature. Some of her works are easily recognizable within the fantasy, horror, and mystery genres, and her latest work may be better classified as hybrids of mystery, gothic, romance, and historical fantasy. Two recent examples, both available in English translation, are the novels *Heart of Tango* (2010) and *The Goldsmith's Secret* (2011).* Her latest recognition came in 2020 when Barceló received Spain's prestigious National Prize for Children's and Young People's Literature for her 2019 novel *El efecto Frankenstein* (The Frankenstein effect).

In Spain, Barceló's influence in the genre was especially felt during the 1980s and 1990s with the publication of three science fiction novels, *Sagrada* (1989; Sacred), *El mundo de Yarek* (1993; Yarek's world), and the novel translated here, *Consecuencias naturales* (1994; *Natural Consequences* [2021]). A prolific short story writer, Barceló has received recognition by fantasy and science fiction critics both in her native country and abroad. Her original short story collection *Futuros peligrosos* (2008; Dangerous futures) is a compilation of fantasy and science fiction stories imagining future technological innovations and their moral and social consequences. An example of Barceló's recent international impact is the fact that *Transfer*, the 2010 film by Damir Lukacevic, was based on one of the short stories included in that collection, "Mil euros por tu vida" (A thousand euros for your life). The English-speaking reader may find one of Barceló's best short stories, 1994's "Estreno," translated as "First Time" in our 2003 science fiction anthology, *Cosmos latinos*.

---

* Please note this introduction contains minor plot spoilers. *Corazón de tango* (2007) and *El secreto del orfebre* (2003)

Natural Consequences and Its Relevance as a Feminist Novel

We chose to make *Natural Consequences* available in English for a number of reasons. First, the novel has stood the test of time. Published in 1994 by Miraguano as part of its "Futuropolis" collection, a second edition appeared in 2019—in time for its twenty-fifth birthday celebration—by Crononauta, an alternative publishing house focusing on science fiction, fantasy, and horror with a gendered perspective. Indeed the novel is a perfect example of how women writers have impacted a genre that has historically been produced by male writers and destined for male audiences. Perhaps a more academic reason for choosing to translate this work is that it illustrates a distinctive trait common to much Spanish science fiction production: the use of satirical, absurd humor based on exaggeration (Molina-Gavilán 2002, 194). Most importantly, the feminist themes Barceló tackles so straightforwardly in this novel are still relevant today.

Natural Consequences opens with the response to a distress call. The human officers and crew of the twenty-third-century space station *Victoria* have learned that a Xhroll cargo ship needs mechanical assistance. The repairs will take some time, and a Xhroll delegation is welcomed aboard the *Victoria*, putting to the test the little that each species knows about the other. One human male, Lieutenant Nico Andrade, is particularly excited by the striking-looking Xhroll visitors—but not by what happens to him after he has sex with one of them. This consequence sets the rest of the story in motion, as Charlie and Ankkhaia, human and Xhroll intelligence officers, race to understand each other's language and customs in order to neutralize threats of extinction, environmental destruction, and interstellar war.

Contemporary readers will quickly recognize the timeliness of the main themes of the novel (revealed in Chapter 2, "Natural Consequences") and the relevance to feminism of concepts now commonly known as inclusive language, toxic masculinity, and female agency. *Natural Consequences* highlights the absurdity of strict patriarchal gender roles, centers agency on female characters, uses humor and satire to decry toxic masculinity, and manipulates language for shock value (among other things), all while telling a provocative and entertaining story.

At first glance, the twenty-third-century setting presents a society where men and women are theoretically equal under the law. Even secondary female characters like Colonel Diana Ortega hold positions of power within the military hierarchy aboard the space station *Victoria*. Significantly, the main female character, Captain Charlie Fonseca, is a confident, independent woman who has a key role in moving the action along, restoring harmony between two worlds, and ultimately saving a pristine natural environment from exploitation. Vanessa Knights (2004, 91) finds that Barceló's stories often give us "female adventurers in space who transgress traditional gender stereotypes." And yet, if the population on the *Victoria* is any guide, then gender equity in this futuristic society is specious, for the station's highest ranking officers are all male, as are two thirds of its crew, and overtly expressed chauvinism, as embodied in Lieutenant Nico Andrade and his group of male friends, is still very much alive and even somewhat tolerated by others.

As for the Xhroll, they are sexually ambiguous hominid beings to whom binary gender categories do not neatly apply, for their society is divided into three groups instead of two, and a Xhroll's reproductive function is not tied to gender identity. And although the Xhroll world seems idyllic, Teresa López-Pellisa

(2019, 257–58) notes that it has a hierarchical class system and rigid gender norms, and practices state repression and reproductive control, which we note includes the silencing of mothers by depriving them of freedom of movement and expression.

Often the only woman writer included in science fiction short story anthologies published in Spain during the this period, Elia Barceló is considered a pioneer in moving the genre away from exclusively masculinist models. It is revealing that when asked about the role of women writers within science fiction circles in the 1990s, Barceló declares that she never felt rejected by male editors or other writers in spite of often being the only woman among them. But she does single out the one instance when she was criticized by male readers because of her gender: when she first published *Natural Consequences*. As she recalls, many of them were offended "because my main character was an overbearing macho prick [. . .] and I use crude language. There were many criticisms and attacks because, since I was a woman, I should focus on pleasanter themes and write in more lyrical prose" (Barceló and Ruiz Garzón 2016). These comments reflect both the larger percentage of male *fandom* in the science fiction scene during the 90s and the patriarchal gender-norm stereotypes still prevalent in Spanish society at that time. López-Pellisa (2019, 273–74) points out that Barceló's novel seems to have touched a nerve, because a visceral comeback to *Natural Consequences* came out in 1995 titled "Machote, machote" (Macho, macho man) in the influential yearly anthology *Visiones*. The story by Ángel Torres Quesada bluntly presents, without subverting its premise, a grotesque world of extreme traditional patriarchal male and female roles and centers on an über–male chauvinist reminiscent of Barceló's Nicodemo Andrade, who delights in raping and ultimately subjugating powerful women. *Natural*

Consequences' subject matter and time frame show that even after centuries of activism and victories (see the space station's name) "macho men" still exist and toxic masculinity has not been made irrelevant. The book presents real feminist concerns as a form of cautionary tale that makes a point to warn against undesirable behaviors such as objectifying, silencing, or raping women while illustrating the moral truth of gender equity.

Today's readers may still fully enjoy Nicodemo Andrade's humiliation and the seemingly vindictive undertones of some of the novel's humor if they understand it as reflecting the style and spirit of the novellas written by Boccaccio and Cervantes. Barceló presents here an exemplary novel for a new feminist age. And her feminist novel also delights in inverting the trope of the one dimensional, "pretty but useless" female characters in most pulp-era science fiction written by male writers. The fact that the male protagonist in *Natural Consequences* doesn't develop as a character despite his seemingly life-altering experience adds to the sweet karma motif. One of the "natural consequences" of Nico's outrageous, outdated machismo is to be demoted to the rank of flat, undeveloped character by the female author who created him.

Language Manipulation in *Natural Consequences*: Translation Challenges

Languages and the complex worldviews they represent are central themes in *Natural Consequences*, as is not uncommon in first-contact science fiction stories. Leticia Gándara Fernández (2016, 80) writes about language and linguistic systems in *Natural Consequences*, arguing they are instruments of social manipulation and thought control that, like in Suzette Haden

Elgin's *Native Tongue* trilogy, are used as means of solving social problems based on gender roles and power structures.

In the world of Barceló's novel, the relationship between language and gender is explored on many levels, often with humor. The disconnect that comes from positioning a binary society alongside a tripartite one, and the confusion caused by inverting the Xhrolls' and humans' physical appearances and reproductive functions, are reflected in the two languages, especially in the use of gender markers. We had to be very sensitive to nuanced gender as we translated and came to appreciate how deftly Barceló was experimenting with inclusive and ambiguous language back in the 1990s.

The centrality of language is established right from the first chapter. When the humans and the Xhroll meet, they communicate by means of automatic translators worn as part of their gear. But the device proves unequal to the complex task of interspecies communication, a fact that prompts Charlie Fonseca and her Xhroll counterpart, Ankkhaia, to spend months working together to learn each other's language and understand their societies' beliefs and practices. As translators ourselves, we felt a special kinship with Ankkhaia and Charlie as we sought to bridge the communication divide the novel presents between Spanish and Xhroll, Spanish and English, males and females.

Language highlights two of *Natural Consequences'* concerns, namely social equity and individual identity. Social equity connects with translation through the use of inclusive language in the novel, while identity resulted in several exciting translation challenges thanks to Barceló's clever manipulation of grammar.

Gender inclusive language was still a controversial, fringe idea in 1996 when Barceló showed how feminism could influence Spanish language conventions, for example by naming males and females separately and distinctly in generalized forms of address rather than always privileging the masculine. Twenty-first-century readers will appreciate how feminism has indeed impacted the Spanish language two centuries before the events in Barceló's novel, since it is becoming commonplace to use inclusive language in public and everyday exchanges, and not only within progressive circles.

Early on in *Natural Consequences* we learn that the crew of the space station *Victoria* uses inclusive language, especially in public, with the implication that this reflects or leads to a more equitable society. In the Spanish they speak, this inclusivity might take the form of a modified swear word, like when Diana Ortega calls Nicodemo Andrade an *hijo de chulo* (son of a pimp), an obvious alteration of *hijo de puta* (son of a bitch) (Molina-Gavilán 2018, 170). Inclusivity is also expressed through gender-marked nouns and adjectives, such as in the speech Commander Kaminsky gives to welcome the Xhroll delegation aboard. We have used italics here to indicate the inclusive language at the opening of his remarks: "Honorables huéspedes del planeta Xhroll. *Todas y todos nosotras y nosotros, ciudadanas y ciudadanos* del planeta Tierra, nos sentimos inmensamente *honradas, honrados y orgullosas, orgullosos* por el raro privilegio que nos ha sido concedido al poder contar con vuestra presencia aquí" (Barceló 2019, 16).

In conventional usage, Spanish defaults to the masculine (*todos*, for example) when there is a mix of genders, but here each gender is explicitly stated and, what is more, the feminine form comes first: *todas* before *todos*, *ciudadanas* before *ciudadanos*. Not only are females no longer subsumed by males, they lead the pack. How best to reproduce this inclusivity in English? The word order, "female and male," was no problem, but sadly we could find no way to do full justice to *todas y todos* or *nosotras y nosotros*, because in English the respective subject pronouns "all" and "we" are neutral for gender. We were pleased, though, that even to today's progressive ear some of the phrases we translated sound a bit unwieldy, such as "We the female and male citizens of Earth" and "Earth's female and male scapegoats." Charlie herself confides to Nico in Chapter 3 that inclusive speech can sometimes feel cumbersome. When talking with him about the fetus, she says, "Speaking of which, why don't we give it a temporary name? So we don't have to always say 'the fetus,' which sounds terrible, or 'he or she,' which, just between us, always sounded super clunky to me, not to mention stupid" (76).

If clunky is how it feels to the characters, then so it should for the readers, too. We made every effort for our translation's inclusive language to mirror when and how it is used in the Spanish original, knowing that at times the phrasing will snag the reader's attention. This snag is a feature not a bug, a nod to the novel's message that it takes collective will, visibility, and a certain amount of personal discomfort to transform a society's cultural norms.

The relationship between language, society, and identity is always powerful and in flux, and in these times when transcending the binary moves into the mainstream in more languages and cultures than ever before, *Natural Consequences* is a timely exercise in speculation. The novel explores the interconnection of language and identity by presenting not just the humans' perspective but the Xhrolls' as well. As Vanessa Knights (1999, 90) observes, "the constructed nature of 'gender' in both societies is evident to the reader and acutely observed by the intelligence officer Charlie Fonseca, whose name is appropriately neither masculine nor feminine. As Fonseca concludes, after contact with the Xhroll, simple binary divisions of both sex and gender break down."

In this passage from Chapter 4, Ankkhaia struggles to understand that humans link gender to reproductive function and codify that relationship through language, specifically through gendered pronouns:

> They constantly use sex in their language. Everything must be either feminine or masculine, even inanimate objects. To refer to people, they must use both possibilities. When speaking in the first person one must choose between them. Humans always know which one to use, but it's hard for me. Am I a *he* or a *she*? The human says I am a woman and must use the feminine form to refer to myself. And yet, within their own sexual framework, the being able to implant life in another being is masculine and the one receiving it is feminine. That, to me, means I am a *he*. However, the two xhri [aliens] agree that I am a *she*. I will have to decide what I'll use for myself and what I'll use to refer to the he-human and the she-human. (89)

Gendered subject pronouns, in fact, became quite a thorny issue for us as translators because they are so much easier to suppress in Spanish than in English, and Barceló employed this strategy to great effect in the text. There are long passages in *Natural Consequences* with few if any grammatical clues to a character's gender identity. Notably, this occurs in scenes featuring only Xhrolls, such as Hithrolgh's council meetings and his conversations with Ankkhaia. Because these passages so cleverly underscore the novel's message about the fluid nature of gender and identity and the possibility of huge paradigm shifts, we wonder if this absence of gendered language is intentional? Is it the equivalent in Xhroll to the inclusive Spanish that the earthlings speak?

Here it is helpful to recall the hierarchy of the three Xhroll social groups. The *abbas* can be implanted, but although procreation is revered, the abbas have very little social power. The *ari-arkhj* are both the implanters and the abbas' protectors, are physically identified by their mysterious breasts, and have some social status. Finally, there are the *xhrea*, who are unable to procreate and are comparatively few in number, but are at the top of the power structure. How does this system map onto gendered language, and how did this affect our work as translators? Although the Xhroll language (as rendered in Spanish) recognizes the existence of different genders—Xhroll characters use both *él* and *ella* (he and she) in reference to specific individuals—only masculine forms are used for the ari-arkhj and the xhrea, whether speaking of them collectively as social groups or referring to individuals such as Ankkhaia and Hithrolgh. All Xhroll are he/him, Xhroll speech suggests, but let's be clear, as rendered in Spanish. We translators never got to work with Xhroll as a source language; we do not know its features. The narrator either translates all but a handful of Xhroll terms into Spanish or simply summarizes or omits the Xhroll speech altogether, as happens in the scene when Charlie and Ankkhaia visit the catacombs of the undead.

Continuing on, the final data point involves the Xhroll abbas. They never take the stage as characters in the novel and are only spoken of as a class that takes the masculine articles *el* and *los*, thus leaving unresolved the question of whether individual abbas would be "he," "she," or something else altogether. Abbas are mothers, and to be a mother is to be powerless in Xhroll society—in the Xhroll language, then, would that be designated by referring to individual abbas as "she"? Though not conclusive evidence, we did find as we pored over the text that on two occasions Xhroll characters whose framework for Nico is based on his alienness and his reproductive role refer to him as "she."

In time, our readings revealed a system governing the use of gender markers in *Natural Consequences*, and we used the following schema to guide us in our work:

- Nico, Charlie, and the other human crewmembers use he/him for those they perceive as male, and she/her for those they perceive as female.
- Ankkhaia uses the masculine when talking to and about other Xhroll. He self-identifies as he/him but accepts that humans, as yet unable to see beyond a vulva and implanted breasts, refer to Xhrolls like himself as she/her.
- The narrator generally reflects the point of view of whichever species or language is dominant in a given scene.

In two or three of the long passages mentioned earlier, not only were subject pronouns in short supply, but other parts of speech also contributed to the ambiguity. In Latin America direct object pronouns are gender marked (*la, lo*, meaning her, him), but Barceló used the more common form in Spain, the unmarked *le*. Similarly, Barceló could opt for the nongendered *su*, a possessive adjective meaning his, her, or its. In one gripping case—gripping for translators, that is—Xhroll characters use the ambiguous *su* in reference to Nico, as an abba. Translating that as "his" or "her" would have been overstepping our role as translators, given the little textual evidence we had about the gender of abbas. After much thought we chose its as the best way to both preserve the ambiguity of the original Spanish and signal the low social status of the abbas.

When we translated *Natural Consequences*, we employed a great deal of linguistic legerdemain to hide or confuse gender whenever we saw that sort of thing happening in the Spanish. Vanessa Knights (2004, 85) has rightly observed that Elia Barceló is "highly conscious of the use and influence of language in conceptualizing and ordering gender relations" and that many of her narratives "focus on the way in which language mediates our experience and shapes our perceptual world." We were therefore pleased but not entirely surprised to receive an email from Barceló confirming our deductions about how language functions in her novel:

> In this novel I did everything possible to create confusion and ambiguity within the range of my language [Spanish]. Sometimes, as you two say, [I did this] by eliminating all possible markers, and at other times by making the pronouns—both subject and direct object—masculine or feminine depending on which character was speaking or thinking, depending on the focus. For example, when Ankkhaia talks with Charlie or thinks something about her, [he says] "he" because [he's] learned that, in the human language, whoever implants life is a "he." (January 9, 2021)*

---

* En esta novela, efectivamente, hice todo lo posible para crear confusión y ambigüedad, dentro de las posibilidades de mi lengua. A veces, como vosotras decís, eliminando en lo posible los marcadores, y en otras ocasiones haciendo que los pronombres tanto de sujeto como de objeto directo sean masculinos o femeninos dependiendo de qué personaje habla o piensa, dependiendo de la focalización. Por ejemplo, cuando Ankhaia [*sic*] habla con Charlie o piensa algo sobre ella, dice "él" porque ha aprendido que quien implanta vida es un "él" en la lengua humana.

This is the Whorfian linguistic determinism that Knights, Gándara Fernández, and others see operating throughout *Natural Consequences*, especially in the final scene, reifying through language the novel's message that gender and identity are social constructs.

Of course, whenever gender markers were explicit in the original Spanish, we used their equivalent in English. But in the end, some confusion remains. It is part of the novel's enduring ability to disorient the reader and disrupt paradigms, and is a natural consequence of the dynamic relationship between language, society, gender, and identity.

REFERENCES

Barceló, Elia. 2003. "First Time." In *Cosmos Latinos: An Anthology of Science Fiction from Latin America and Spain*, edited by Andrea L. Bell and Yolanda Molina-Gavilán, 235–42. Middletown, CT: Wesleyan University Press.

———. 2019. *Consecuencias naturales*. Madrid: Crononauta.

Barceló, Elia, and Ricard Ruiz Garzón. 2016. "Elements of the Fantastic: Elia Barceló and Ricard Ruiz Garzón in Conversation." Translated by Lawrence Schimel. *Strange Horizons*, October 31, 2016. http://strangehorizons.com/non-fiction/articles/elements-of-the-fantastic.

Gándara Fernández, Leticia. 2016. "Análisis de los procedimientos lingüísticos en *Consecuencias naturales* de Elia Barceló." *Anuario de Estudios Filológicos*, vol. 39: 79–90.

Heredia, Daniel. 2014. "Elia Barceló: '¿Mi motivación para escribir? El placer. Sencillamente me gusta hacerlo y me divierte mucho.'" *A los libros* (blog), November 17, 2014. https://aloslibros.com/

elia-barcelo-mi-motivacion-para-escribir-el-placer-sencillamente-me-gusta-hacerlo-y-me-divierte-mucho.

Knights, Vanessa. 1999. "'Taking a Leap beyond Epistemological Boundaries: Spanish Fantasy / Science Fiction and Feminist Identity Politics." *Paragraph: A Journal of Modern Critical Theory* 22, no. 1: 76–94.

———. 2004. "Transformative Identities in the Science Fiction of Elia Barceló: A Literature of Cognitive Estrangement." In *Reading the Popular in Contemporary Spanish Texts*, edited by Shelley Godsland and Nickianne Moody, 74–99. Newark: University of Delaware Press.

López-Pellisa, Teresa. 2019. "Epílogo: Naturales (in)consecuencias." In *Consecuencias naturales*, by Elia Barceló, 257–75. Madrid: Crononauta.

Molina-Gavilán, Yolanda. 2002. *Ciencia ficción en español: Una mitología moderna ante el cambio*. Lewiston, NY: Edwin Mellen.

———. 2018. "Narrativa 1980–2000." In *Historia de la ciencia ficción en la cultura española*, edited by Teresa López-Pellisa, 151–76. Estudios de la cultura española 43. Madrid: Vervuert/Iberoamericana.

AUTHOR'S NOTE

This novel and I owe much to the thousands of hours of conversation and of life that I have shared over the years with the people closest to me. Conversations about men and women, about human beings. Life experiences concerning behaviors, feelings, examples, opinions.

I would like to express my gratitude to every one of them.*

I wrote this novel twenty-five years ago, and it worries me that we've hardly made any progress in all this time.

I dedicate this novel to all the women and all the men who work every day toward the goal of reaching equality, of building a world where we may all support each other and commit to the creation of a common future world of peace, parity, and respect; a world where violence, exploitation, and stupidity will be a thing of the past.

E. B.

---

* Translators' Note: The original Spanish for them here, ellas has a feminine gender marker that agrees with the noun personas. The author relishes in pointing out parenthetically that she uses the feminine ending only because it is grammatically correct: (Me refiero a personas, de ahí el femenino), (I'm talking about people, hence the feminine.)

NATURAL CONSEQUENCES

NEW FRIENDSHIPS

CONTACT

"They're going to land? They're going to land *here*?" Diego's voice wavered between stunned and disbelieving, salted with excitement and peppered with doubt.

Igor, a junior communications engineer, nodded, his tense facial muscles expressing the same range of emotions Diego had with his words.

"Looks like they've got a minor insulation problem in their hold, or whatever the Xhroll equivalent of a cargo bay is. Nothing serious, but we're the closest station to them and since officially we're on good terms . . ."

"But no one's really ever had direct contact with them."

"We'll have the honor of being first, then. The commander has already given the okay."

"Are they all males?"

The five officers gathered in the comm room burst out laughing. Nico was simply beyond help. He was a great mechanic and, as he often said, his heart—if he had one—belonged to his machines, especially the mini bots in charge of exterior fixes to the ships and stations. But what he'd also amply demonstrated during shore leaves was that women held second place, maybe not in his heart but rather a foot or so below.

"Jeez, come on, guys. It's a serious question. Are there any women? We haven't seen fresh meat in ages."

"There are seventy-three female crewmembers on this station, Nico," Hal replied softly.

"Yeah, right. And two hundred and fourteen guys. Besides, I'm not talking about female crewmembers, I'm talking about women."

"Fresh meat," mocked Diego.

"If Colonel Ortega hears you, you're up shit creek, Mister Macho." Igor'd had a few run-ins with Diana Ortega after he'd left the required feminine endings off adjectives in written communiques to the crew.

"Well, are there or aren't there?"

Igor showed him a printout. "Here's the complete list of the officers on board the *Harrkh*. The last five are the ones who'll visit our facilities and interact with us. If you can figure anything out from this list . . ."

Nico eagerly grabbed the sheet of paper while Hal and Diego looked over his shoulder.

The printer had written fifty lines of what looked like a random sequence of letters, mostly consonants.

"No one on Earth could figure this out."

"That's what I mean."

"This is a joke. No way are these their names."

"It's just a phonetic approximation for our benefit, Nico." Hal, a linguist, was the senior communications officer.

"OK, great. So how are we supposed to find out if women are coming aboard?"

"By waiting for the commander to introduce them to us. When they take off their spacesuits it'll probably be obvious who's what. Assuming they have females, of course."

"Of course they have females. Haven't you guys seen the newsfeeds? And wow, what women! If they're even half as hot as the chick who made first contact . . ."

"But maybe females don't serve on cargo ships. They say they have a population shortage."

"If they're as like us as they say, they'll have no fucking choice but to bring women along. For equal rights and stuff."

"Ok, men, I'm going to go pretty myself up a bit." Nico ran his hand over his regulation-shaved chin and stood up. "Gotta make a good first impression on the ladies, especially when they're aliens."

"Hey, Nico." Diego's face showed his apprehension. "You're not thinking of screwing a Xhroll, are you?"

Nico gave a wolfish grin, an almost offensive display of perfectly white teeth.

"Only with their consent, I swear. Gotta hoist our banners high!"

Their reactions ran the standard range from guffaws and backslapping to Diego's look of horror and Hal's smiling but worried face.

"What if they're monsters in disguise?"

Nico burst out laughing.

"You've been watching too many B movies, Dieguito."

"And if you get her pregnant?"

Controlling the smile at the corner where his trim mustache met his mouth, Nico counted off on his fingers:

"One, in spite of them looking like us, I don't think we're that compatible. Two, I've never known a woman who was fertile without the aid of the right pharmaceuticals. And three, maybe I'd be doing them a favor. Didn't you say their world is underpopulated?"

And with that, Nico made his triumphant exit while his shipmates roared.

Two hours later, the officers of the *Victoria*, Earth's most remote space station, were assembled in Reception Hall wearing dress uniforms. Among whispers and repressed chuckles, they waited for the alien delegation to arrive. Commander Kaminsky, a Lithuanian of Polish descent who seemed made of barbed wire, furtively checked his portable translator every twenty seconds and pulled at the lower hem of his formal flight jacket.

This would be his first face-to-face encounter with beings from another world, and even though he knew they looked very human, he was considerably unnerved. What's more, he wasn't at all sure that the device the senior communications officer had clipped onto his belt really worked. Kaminsky, along with every other well-informed citizen, knew that two years ago the *Pallas Atenea* had established first contact with the Xhroll people and that a small group of linguists from both worlds had spent a lot of time designing a functional language that enabled basic communication. He knew that, but now that he was on the verge of using the language himself he found his confidence in the linguists' work running low.

In response to an acoustic signal, the men and women of the *Victoria* stood at attention while the opening strains of the terrestrial anthem played and the Xhroll delegation proceeded up the center aisle, led by the Catholic chaplain to whom fell the delicate job of master of ceremonies, the general opinion being that this way, after five years of service, the poor man could tell the bishop that he had on one occasion been useful.

Nico, who had managed to snag a perfect spot along the aisle in the forward third of the hall, watched out of the corner of his eye as the Xhroll approached the dais. His excitement grew, along with the rising tone of countless surprised murmurs. Even if there was just one woman among them, one single woman, she would be his. He no longer cared how ugly she might be. What mattered was that he'd be the first human to . . .

The sight of the Xhroll left him breathless and amazed. They were . . . they were . . . beautiful. They were perfect. So perfect that for an instant, just for an instant, he didn't know or care whether they were male or female. They all had different skin tones and hair color and were simply dressed in unadorned black jumpsuits. Their body types were so similar that only after they'd ascended the dais with the commander and turned to face the *Victoria*'s officers could Nico be certain that the second Xhroll from the left was female. The size of her breasts, though not excessive, removed all doubt. The rest of the crew was male. All other differences were minimal: the Xhroll all appeared young, strong, and agile, and the muscles of their faces were relaxed, doll-like. The shape and color of their eyes, the cut of their hair, and the color of their skin made it seem easy to tell them apart, but that was a misleading impression because, except for those details, the five of them were virtually interchangeable.

The commander began his speech while the Xhroll swept the room with their eyes, not a single facial movement betraying their reactions.

"Honorable guests from the planet Xhroll. We, the female and male citizens of Earth, feel proud and deeply honored by the rare privilege of your presence here today. We extend to you our full hospitality and solemnly pledge to do everything in our power to ensure that your journey continues in safety and that the friendly relations between our two species strengthen and prosper over time.

On behalf of the female and male citizens of Earth, I welcome you most cordially to the space station *Victoria*."

Nico's eyes never left the female Xhroll's face during Commander Kaminsky's speech; now, though, he had been spotted. The alien's gaze locked with his during her sweep of the room and lingered for a few seconds. Ignoring the regulations, Nico flashed her his radiant smile, the undoing of so much prior female resistance.

Her eyes had left his to continue wandering, but came back to him. Nico thought he saw in her impassive face the beginnings of a reaction he couldn't quite name.

Then the audience began applauding the commander and the contact broke.

One of the Xhroll, the dark-skinned one, stepped forward and the tiny translator brought his words to the officers over the hall's loudspeakers.

"Men of planet Earth, Xhroll thanks you. We have no interest in future contact, but your help was needed now. And we will help you if you ever need it."

The message was so short and the ending so curt that, for a moment, no one knew what to do. After a few silent seconds the chaplain began to applaud and was immediately joined by the commander; then the entire audience began to clap, whistle, and roar with such fervor that it started to feel ridiculous even to them and the applause abruptly stopped.

The crowd broke up and headed over to the long tables that lined the wall and served as the bar. Knowing that the aliens would be monopolized by the ranking officers for the first hour or so, and confident that no one would beat him to his goal, Nico went to pour himself a cup of synthetic wine. As he did, he found himself facing Diana Ortega, who was reaching for the same pitcher.

"They're a people of few words, eh Colonel?"

"Few and downright rude ones, Lieutenant."

"Don't you want to go meet the men and the women? At least the woman?"

The colonel took a long swig from her plastic cup.

"Bet you didn't even bat an eye when that son of a bastard said 'men' instead of 'men and women.'"

"Well, Colonel, maybe they're different. And you know, a few centuries ago the people of Earth didn't care if 'everyone' included both men and women either."

Ortega snorted.

"I don't see how that's funny. Anyhow, what about you, don't you want to be introduced to the female?"

The colonel and the lieutenant got along pretty well, in spite of the gap in rank and Nico's reputation as a womanizer. Nico figured that was actually why they got along, but Ortega thought it was because, in any self-contained community, the jester always has a role to play.

"That's my plan, Colonel. You must understand, I'm honor bound."

Ortega threw her head back, her laughter sounding like a lion's roar.

"You're a son of a pimp, Andrade. Go on, give it a try. Maybe for once you'll meet your match. I doubt it, though. Any woman who's not bothered by that kind of treatment . . . Aw whatever, I don't want to be a pain. Lemme know how it goes."

The colonel disappeared into the crowd and Nico elbowed his way toward the rear table where the aliens' remarkable height and black outfits made them stand out. Their voices sounded soft, pleasant, and mysteriously impersonal through the translator—and because of that, exciting.

Nico was still mulling over which of his many approaches to try when, before he could make a move, the woman broke away from the group and approached until she stood before him.

"Are you looking for me?" he heard her ask.

His mouth suddenly went dry; he had guessed she'd be on the timid side and his instincts rarely failed him like this.

"You and only you," he answered, looking into her eyes six inches above his and ignoring the fact that she'd been the one to start the conversation.

"You are the only terrestrial who attracts me. The others are not clear."

"What do you mean," asked Nico, intrigued.

"Either they don't know what they want, or they know but don't express it. Your personal relations must be exhausting."

"Because neither males nor females ever know what the other thinks or wants?"

"Exactly."

"Well, don't you believe it. We have our protocols. Men and women always think we know. Or we guess and of course get it wrong."

"That strikes me as needlessly complicated."

"It's a matter of what you're used to."

"Why did you contact me?"

If Nico had been able to blush he would have, right then and there.

"Well, I wanted . . . um . . . I wanted to have sex with you, if that's possible and you agree."

The Xhroll cupped the ear holding the translator, as if checking that it was working correctly.

That did it, thought Nico, *I've gone too far. Now she'll get all offended and I'll have just started an intergalactic diplomatic incident.*

"My translator tells me you used a past tense. Does that mean that sex was your initial intention but you are no longer interested?"

Nico shook his head, confused. They were creepily literal!

"Yes, no, . . . Yes, of course I'm still interested. What about you?"

"I am, too, but I must get clearance. You can get yours while I get mine. We'll meet at the door in five minutes."

She turned and set off toward the group of Xhroll, leaving Nico frozen to the spot. Five minutes. In five minutes he had to talk with Kaminsky and meet back up with her. No way was there enough time. Besides, what the hell did he have to get clearance from Kaminsky for? He wasn't on duty, and he could do whatever he felt like during his free time; if this were a human female it would be ridiculous to ask his commander for permission to sleep with her, so why do it just because it was a Xhroll? Most likely Kaminsky would turn white with rage, his usual reaction to anything that disturbed his routine, and he'd have Nico sent to lock-up until the visitors left. But if Kaminsky didn't find out until *afterward,* sure, he could punish Nico for what he did or for telling him after the fact, but he couldn't actually prevent anything.

Once he made his decision he headed toward the door, his throat tight and his stomach in knots, though through years of habit his bright smile and the way he walked disguised how he was really feeling. He wasn't regretting what he and the Xhroll had agreed to. No way. This was going to make him the most famous guy in the Fleet and his reputation would be legendary, no doubt about that. His apprehension came from suddenly remembering that in their brief conversation the woman's icy facial expression had never changed, as if her muscles were incapable of anything but speech, and he realized that she didn't excite him. She was good-looking, tall, young, and well proportioned, and had beautiful, long blonde hair and eyes like green crystals, but she was as cold as ice, at least in public. If things didn't change in private, he was going to have to fire up his imagination in order to do what he'd planned. For the first time in his thirty-five years, the specter of temporary impotence crossed his mind, but it was just a fleeting thought that he quickly banished. That wasn't going to happen to him. There was no fucking way. He was going to screw that Xhroll if it was the last thing he did.

Igor and Diego were standing near the door when he got there, each with a cup in hand.

"Don't tell me you're giving up to go cry your heart out in defeat?" Igor teased.

"Maybe he's finally gotten some common sense." Diego's scornful expression contradicted his words.

His friends' jokes restored Nico's flagging courage. He glanced at his watch and then back at the room before answering:

"These Xhroll women, they're not only hot, they're super punctual."

And indeed, the woman was making a beeline for them through knots of men and women who parted before her.

"All set," she said when she arrived.

He took her delicately by the elbow, causing the first expression he'd seen on her face, something he took to be surprise though it might have been anything, and winking back at his shipmates, he left the hall.

When Igor and Diego recovered from their surprise they saw that practically every officer filling the hall had their eyes glued to the door through which Nico and the woman had disappeared. The four Xhroll and the commander anxiously scanned the faces around them, though their posture was relaxed.

From somewhere in the back of the room came a whistle and some applause and soon everyone was clapping, laughing, joking, and exchanging fist bumps.

The four Xhroll didn't go quite that far, but fleeting yet unmistakable smiles crossed their impassive faces.

Only two people remained deadly serious: Commander Kaminsky and the Catholic chaplain.

The corridors leading from the main hall to his officer's cubicle, which Nico proudly called "my apartment," had never seemed so long. If they'd been on Earth, his strategy would have been clear: a drink, a good candlelit dinner with soft background music, a biplane ride over the mountains, a perfect landing on his building's rooftop, a moonlight dip in the heated pool, a glass of champagne in front of the fire . . . a commonplace strategy indeed, but one that brought results. But on board the *Victoria* . . . what could one offer an alien on the *Victoria*? Five square meters and a rickety fold-down bed.

He thought maybe he should have asked Kaminsky to let him use his quarters. Rumor had it that, despite his monastic appearance, the commander slept on an eiderdown-covered double bed. He could have claimed that it wouldn't be for his own sake but rather for his exotic visitor's. Although Kaminsky could have answered that a human male was just a human male and he himself could show the Xhroll woman how things were done on Earth. Nico imagined Kaminsky taking off his long johns and almost burst into laughter.

He would have to make do without candles, silks, or eiderdown comforters. The only thing he had was a prime quality body, and the Xhroll would have to settle for that. After all, their species didn't seem to be very prone to romance. Bet they didn't find that "clear" enough.

He inserted his badge in the slot and the door opened and closed behind them.

She took the translator off her belt and put in on the bedside table while making sure the left earbud was still on. He flashed her his radiant smile once more since, for the time being, he didn't quite know what to do or say.

"Do you take off your clothes to copulate here?" she asked, her hand poised on the zipper of her black jumpsuit.

"Yes, of course." The chick was incredibly direct. "You don't in your world?"

"We do. But other peoples don't."

Other peoples. She had said other peoples. Therefore, the Xhroll were in contact with other nonhuman species, and not just in contact but they also seemed to have sexual intercourse with them.

That's why the chick took things so casually, because it wasn't the first time for her. Who knows how many fairly monstrous aliens had already screwed her. Not that he expected her to be a virgin, of course, but he'd imagined this would be the first time for both of them and, actually, as it turned out, he was the virgin. He didn't like that idea one bit. He wasn't used to being made a fool of in that area, that's for sure. Maybe the chick added a notch on her belt every time she screwed an alien. The thought put a crooked smile on his face: that was just what he had done for the last twenty years, and what he planned on doing as soon as she left his apartment after the 6:00 a.m. call. *Don't be sexist*, he told himself. *If you do it, why shouldn't she?*

The Xhroll had taken off her jumpsuit and was folding it carefully on the floor. She wasn't wearing any type of underwear and her skin was white and smooth, with ivory undertones. When she stood back up and turned to face him he saw that she lacked any body hair and her genitals were so bare they seemed more clinical than lewd. Her nipples and her vulva were of the same exact color as the rest of her skin, which made her look like a twentieth-century mannequin in a window display.

Nico swallowed and began taking off his clothes while she looked at him impassively, her arms relaxed.

He'd always been proud of his bulging muscles, his tan skin, a fine gold chain glittering flirtatiously on his hairy chest. And yet he felt stupid under that icy gaze, as if his body were a freak show. It took him a few seconds to decide to take off his boxer shorts, which could hardly hide his erection. What if the men on her planet weren't built like that? What if she'd never seen a penis before? And what if, much worse, she was used to bigger penises that were double or triple the size of his?

He forced himself to banish any thoughts that would decrease the sexual tension. Before that could happen, he quickly took off his shorts and freed his legs with a fluid move perfected over years of practice.

She kept looking at him with an expression that was, in fact, a lack of expression.

Nico swore under his breath. He felt ridiculous, absurd and passive, as if he were waiting for her to take the initiative, as if suddenly he didn't see himself capable of doing what he'd set out to do.

Casting aside all thoughts, he stepped toward her, slipped his arm around her waist, and drew her toward him. The woman was warm and her skin was soft. Nico breathed a sigh of relief. Somewhere in his subconscious he had expected and feared finding cold reptilian skin. He held her even closer and, standing almost on tiptoe, started kissing her neck and ear, simulating a passion he was still far from feeling. But he knew that if he kept on forcing himself to breathe and let himself go by stroking her skin, sooner or later his desire would be real. It was only a matter of time.

Her hands started to explore his back, literally muscle by muscle, from the nape of his neck to the farthest part of his thighs, as if she was taking inventory, like a masseuse trying to determine her patient's general state of health.

Nico began to fantasize with a purpose, trying to forget her exploration, turning it into something desirable and exciting. He searched for her lips, which she kept closed for a while before finally realizing what the man expected from her. Then she suddenly opened her mouth, and Nico had the dizzying feeling that the besieged castle he was trying to conquer had now become a bottomless pit that would end up swallowing him whole. Breathless and out of control, he pulled away from her open mouth and, to hide his awkwardness, dragged her onto the bed in an effort to turn his fit of fear into a frenzy of passion. She let herself go, her sparkling eyes remaining open and vigilant.

"Can't you close your eyes?" he asked.

"Of course I can. What for?"

"We humans think we can intensify the feeling that way."

"I can try."

The Xhroll closed her eyes and Nico felt a bit better while concentrating on her breasts, tenaciously licking her nipples, trying without success to make them hard.

"Do you like that?" he asked after a while.

"Yes," she said without opening her eyes. "It's pleasant."

Shit! thought Nico. *Pleasant. The damn woman finds it pleasant. Not a sigh, not a gasp, not even a miserly muscle spasm. She might as well be visiting a waste recycling plant. All that's missing is for her to say it's "interesting."*

He decided to skip the preliminaries. When all was said and done, the chick wasn't human. What a human woman thought of as necessary foreplay, she seemed to just see as nonsense, a stupid childish game. Maybe a bit of brute force would snap her out of that composure of hers that was driving him crazy.

He violently pulled her legs apart and got himself ready to penetrate her.

He immediately regretted it.

A first glance at her white, open vulva reminded him he'd never taken a woman without touching her there first. It might be a superstition, but it was one that was too ingrained to be dismissed just like that, so fighting a hint of disgust, he placed his hand between the Xhroll's legs and almost took it away again, scared. The woman secreted a type of viscous substance that must correspond to a human's vaginal discharge, but it had an acrid smell, almost vomit-like, and it stuck to his fingers with unusual persistence. What if she was also different inside? What if all those *vagina dentata* myths had some truth behind them after all? Humans knew practically nothing about the Xhroll. What if . . .?

"I want to warn you that I'm not taking any contraceptive measures," she suddenly informed him, using the same tone of voice used over the loudspeakers at spaceports.

"Do you want me to take care of it?"

"I just want you to know."

"Ok. Wait a minute."

He jumped out of bed, trying to figure out what to do next. It was almost the first time something like that had happened to him. Practically all human women were voluntarily barren until they decided to invert the situation and take medicine to make them fertile again. In the old days there were some rubber sheaths that fitted onto the penis and kept male semen from entering the woman's uterus, but he was certain that not one of those prehistoric inventions was to be found anywhere on the *Victoria*. They were on board a space station, not in a museum.

So then, what? Confess he hadn't anticipated that possibility and end the night sleeping together like brother and sister? No. That would be too stupid.

He opened the only drawer he had and began to look through its contents, knowing he would find nothing that could remotely serve as a contraceptive. He could call sickbay and ask if they had something, but that would hurt his reputation too much. He would have to keep looking.

Suddenly he found something that could work.

He took an aspirin out of its wrapper, turned to the woman so she could clearly see what he was doing, and dry-swallowed it. He smiled toward the Xhroll once again, lowered the lighting, and got ready to finish what he'd started.

Seated facing the large windows in Olympia Hall, one of the three recreational areas with a view to the outside, Igor, Hal,

and Diego watched the Xhroll spacecraft as it was being prepared for takeoff. They were impatiently waiting for Nico to
join them and provide a complete report on the previous night.
The three of them were on dayshift and only had forty minutes
before reporting for duty, but they were ready to risk being late
to their posts if that meant finding out what had gone down
in Nico's cubicle, and what was going on in the commander's
office, where he was at that moment.

The *Victoria*'s insulation specialists had solved the *Harrkh*'s
problem much faster than everyone thought because, apparently,
they'd just had to modify a few terrestrial spare parts so they
matched the alien spacecraft's requirements. Nobody really knew
why the Xhroll lacked the necessary spare parts for their own
maintenance and repair, but there was that old joke going around,
the one about how a Rolls-Royce owner doesn't need invoices for
repairs since, officially, a Rolls-Royce never breaks down. Another
joke du jour was the one about the Xhroll having Japanese blood.
When something goes wrong the answer is for everyone to commit ritual suicide. But their blood must have been tainted with
Latin blood, which forced them to resort to the Band-Aid solution
to save their own hides or, more accurately, to save the cargo,
meaning they may have some Scottish blood as well.

The three officers had stayed up practically all night, strolling
around all the recreational areas, mingling with different groups,
cracking jokes, and speculating about options that became ever
more absurd as the alcohol and exhaustion levels rose. They
finally ended up at Nico's cubicle door waiting to be the first to
congratulate the champion or to "solemnly pick up the pieces,"
in Diego's words. And yet Kaminsky had gotten there first.

The minute the door opened to let out the Xhroll, as cool
and fresh as she'd been ten hours earlier, and Nico, exhausted

and smiling, Colonel Aichinger had been there with security to escort the two of them to the commander's office. Nico and his buddies barely had time to exchange quick looks and make a couple of gestures understood by all: "Olympia Hall. We'll be there."

And there they were, half-heartedly sipping their alt.café and glancing alternately at the door where Nico had to come in once Kaminsky was finished with him, and at the window where they could see the spaceship that would take the Xhroll woman away.

"I wonder if he's fallen in love with her," said Diego in his best killjoy voice.

He was answered by his shipmates' roaring laughter and Nico's slap on his shoulder.

"Let's cut the mush, Dieguito. The Xhroll aren't romantic in the least, I'm telling you."

They all stood up and immediately sat back down again once Nico had settled into an easy chair, his back to the window.

"What did Kaminsky want?" asked Hal.

"You're really something, buddy! I've got a ton of interesting stuff to tell you, only fifteen minutes to spill it all, and all you want to know is what did the Big Boss want. Oh, well! He basically wanted the same thing you do, but resigned himself to making sure we're both still alive and the Xhroll has no complaints."

"And what about you?"

"Apparently he doesn't care if I'm satisfied or not."

"And are you?"

"Am I what? Satisfied?" he cracked a randy, dreamy smile whose purpose was to increase the tension as they waited. Well, gentlemen. The truth is I am."

"Come on, man! Tell us!"

Nico eased back in the chair, crossed his hands behind his neck and just lay there, smiling wordlessly.

"C'mon everyone, let's go!" said Igor standing up. "Don Juan isn't feeling chatty."

"Shit, guys, don't be that way! The thing is, I don't know where to start . . . It'd be easier if you asked me questions."

Igor sat back down.

Meanwhile a bunch of people who were trying to go unnoticed while clinging to Nico's every word had been inching closer.

"Let's see," Hal started. "What's her body like?"

"You've already seen that. She's a babe."

"Yeah, alright, but is she normal?"

"She has no tentacles or antennae or anything weird if that's what you mean. Mind you, she's white all over."

"All over?" Several voices asked the question.

Nico nodded while taking a sip of Diego's coffee.

"Every millimeter. No part of her is differently colored."

"Active or passive?" Igor asked with interest.

"Well, at first she was kind of passive. What am I saying, kind of? She was as passive as a chunk of marble. But then . . . then she started getting into it, and then she almost ate me up."

He concealed the last comment behind one of his smiles so no one could perceive the images suddenly flooding his brain: the Xhroll on top, riding him like a jockey on a wild horse while he fought with all of his strength to free himself of a body that was sealed unnaturally onto his own. The Xhroll with her head between his legs sucking him brutally, painfully, holding him so tightly that he couldn't manage to tear away. The Xhroll shooting a succession of electric shocks all through his skin that left him breathless and made him yell out in anger and pain. He shut off the memories streaming through his mind and asked Diego to bring him another coffee.

"And, listen, did the chick . . .?" Igor realized there were several females among the people listening to him and reformulated his question just as a few eyebrows were being arched. "Did you both manage to climax?"

Nico brought as much drama as he could into looking offended.

"Of course."

"How many times?" asked an anonymous voice.

"I don't really know. I lost count after the fifth time."

Once again, memories washed over his moment of triumph in Olympia Hall. That burning feeling in his lower belly, like a trail of lit gunpowder, like an acid corroding the insides of his body. Once, twice, he couldn't remember how many times, that much was true. The pain that left him blind for a few moments, howling with fear. And her, staring with delirious intensity at his pain-disfigured face, her eyes open, pale as death, breathing slowly and heavily, as if drinking in his panic.

His coffee arrived and he drank it down in one gulp, burning his tongue.

Then the six o'clock watch rang and, grudgingly, everyone started to get up.

"Should we go?" asked Diego who worked only three halls away from the miniaturized robotics workshop.

Nico shook his head.

"I have to go to sickbay. Orders from Kaminsky. Xhrolls are clean as far as airborne contagions go, but apparently nobody had foreseen this kind of close encounter."

Igor, Hal, Diego, and Nico walked together toward the door

and went down the first corridor, surrounded by people taking different paths. Once they reached the point where they had to go their separate ways, Nico, following a sudden impulse, shoved them into a corner and, after making sure no one could hear, told them about the aspirin. Somehow that made him feel better, as if vindicated in part for everything that he'd gone through and would never be able to admit.

"Not a word to anyone, ok? If they find out upstairs, they'll hang me from my thumbs."

He wagged his aforementioned thumbs, stuck them in his belt, and strolled toward sickbay, whistling out of tune.

NATURAL CONSEQUENCES

Commander Kaminsky welcomed the medical captain into what he called his workroom, a sort of living room cum informal office located next to his sleeping quarters. Kaminsky, not quite smiling, which would have disturbed the doctor too much, allowed his lips to curve up slightly when he saw him arrive.

"Make yourself at home, Captain. I just got some great news and thought we could allow ourselves a glass of sherry to celebrate." He turned to a small cupboard and took out a bottle and two crystal wine glasses. "I just got the last message from the *Harrkh* before they make the initial jump on the journey home. The hold has been secured and they are sure it will withstand the jump. The officers who came over are perfectly healthy and they thank us once again." He poured sherry in both glasses, handed one to the captain and sat down facing him, glass in hand.

"You know something?" he added. "These last few weeks, ever since this damned visit started, I've been afraid there'd be an incident, don't ask me what type because I don't even know myself; something that would put us in an awkward position.

I don't know, a fight between two officers, a flu epidemic that would turn out to be lethal for them, who knows? . . . I probably read too much fiction. The thing is that even Lieutenant Andrade's folly turned out to be harmless. As it happens, it may even help to strengthen our relations which, as you know, haven't been too friendly until now."

Kaminsky lowered his gaze from the ceiling, noticed the captain hadn't made the slightest remark and only then realized the *Victoria*'s chief medical officer must have a problem, and a big one at that, because everyone knew better than to bother the commander with trifles.

"Is anything the matter, Roland?"

The captain placed his glass on the table between them and ran both hands through his thinning hair.

"Something is the matter, sir. The problem is, I don't quite know what."

"You wouldn't be talking about an epidemic, would you?" Kaminsky, no longer relaxed, looked like a wire puppet again.

"No, sir. Fortunately not. Lieutenant Andrade seems to be the only victim for now, which isn't strange given the circumstances."

"An alien virus? That's what I was afraid of, but does it affect our people?"

"I have no idea. I've given him every medical test we have available, every test our technology has to offer and, I must confess, I don't know what's wrong with him."

"Will he have to be sent home?"

"I'm not sure. I can't predict how the disease will develop and I have no way of knowing if he would survive the trip back to Earth."

"Is he really that sick?"

Mathieu Roland ran his hand through his hair again, looking hesitant.

"No, he isn't too sick. He just suffers from minor but constant discomfort. Frequent nausea, stomach cramps, general weakness, dizziness, minor depression, sensitivity to light. A lot of minor symptoms that don't point to a clear diagnosis."

"So what do you suggest we do?"

"I thought we might consult with the *Harrkh*'s medical officer. If it's a Xhroll disease they would be in the best position to treat it."

Kaminsky's lips tightened into a thin line.

"Of course, it's only a suggestion. But if they are about to make the jump, we'd have to make a decision . . ."

"Quickly, I know."

"Sorry, Commander."

Kaminsky got up.

"I will inform you when I make my decision. Meanwhile, I assume you've ordered Andrade to go into quarantine."

"Yes, of course, sir. He and his closest male friends are in isolation. As far as females, though, it's a bit harder, sir. You're familiar with the lieutenant's . . . habits."

Kaminsky's face had become a stony mask.

"Have him make a complete list of every female crewmember he has come in contact with during these last few weeks. A complete list, no matter what rank, occupation, or marital status. This is not the time to worry about acting like gentlemen."

"Yes, sir."

After Captain Roland left, Kaminsky banged his desk hard with his fist, then locked himself in the bathroom and sat on the toilet to think about whether to contact the *Harrkh*.

In a small four-bed room in sickbay, Igor, Hal, and Diego were halfheartedly playing dice. They had been under observation for five days, and although none of them had shown any symptoms, the chief medical officer had told the three of them they would have to remain in lockdown for two to three more weeks until Nico's disease could be positively diagnosed.

The first two days had been terrifying, because any minor ache was instantly interpreted as a manifestation of the strange alien disease. Diego got a pimple on his chin a few hours into quarantine, and for a few minutes, his two mates had pressed up against the wall, as far away from him as the room's few square meters of space allowed, pushing the call button like crazy and looking at Diego as if he were about to turn into an old-fashioned movie monster. After a while, once the medical team had laid their fears about the pimple to rest, relations resumed their normal course, and five days in, their biggest issue wasn't fear but total and complete boredom.

"Have you guys seen that mid-twentieth-century movie *Alien*?" asked Diego while Hal tallied up the points.

"Flat films? I don't know how you can stand to watch them, Diego. What's it about?"

"It's about some humans on a cargo ship who land on an unexplored planet and some kind of octopus jumps onto one of their faces and sticks to his helmet."

"Fuck!" whispered Igor.

"And then they take him up to the ship, put him in quarantine, and think he's going to die, but all of a sudden the bug falls off his face. The guy recovers and he's starving, and while he's eating and talking to his teammates, blood spews from his mouth, he starts having convulsions, and some sort of snake comes out of his stomach and splits him open."

"Fuck, Diego! You really have bad taste!" said Hal, rubbing his own stomach.

"I just can't stop thinking about that movie. What if what's ailing Nico is something like that? What if that Xhroll laid an egg inside him and a monster's gonna come out of him?"

Igor got up from the table with a stern look on his face.

"If you go on talking about stuff like that, I'll bash your face in and ask to be put in isolation. I don't know about the rest of you, but I have enough trouble dealing with the situation as it is without having to think about that kind of shit."

At that exact moment the door opened and everyone automatically checked their watches. It wasn't time to eat or have any kind of medical checkup, although one never knew if some member of the medical team had thought of a new test to try out on them. Unconsciously, they backed up against the wall, their palms sweaty.

Captain Roland entered the room not wearing an isolation suit.

"Guys, gather your stuff. Quarantine is over."

"Do they know what it is Nico has, Captain?"

"Yes, we think so. And don't worry, it's not contagious. You may return to your normal routines."

"Could you tell us what he's got?"

Roland looked up at the ceiling, as if trying to orient himself on an invisible map, then looked down at the tip of his shoes.

"I'm not authorized to tell, I'm sorry. You'll have to ask him."

"Can we see him?"

"You'll have to ask Dr. Marinetti about that"

The three of them looked worriedly at each other. Marinetti was a civilian who had been awarded the rank of lieutenant by the Fleet so that he could join the *Victoria* as a psychiatrist.

"Is he that sick?"

"I can't tell you anything."

Nico's friends picked up their stuff and, as they were leaving, Roland spoke again.

"Andrade will need a lot of moral support from now on, gentlemen. If you are his true friends, go see Marinetti. He'll tell you how you should act."

They lingered for a few minutes but, since the captain wasn't about to add anything else, they said goodbye and left sickbay while puzzling over every possible illness that would need that kind of treatment: progressive paralysis, some type of cancer that would disfigure his face . . .

In the meantime, Nico was laying across the bed in one of the few single rooms in sickbay, sobbing into a pillow that was as unresponsive to his tears as to his punches.

Dr. Marinetti's waiting room was empty. A space station's personnel is carefully chosen with regard to their mental health and, whenever an issue does come up, almost everyone prefers to talk to a good friend or use one of the psych therapy machines instead of confiding in a perfect stranger. That was why, people said, both the chaplain and the psychiatrist had reserved one of the ten therapy machines for their own use. They felt lonely and useless.

That was probably another reason Marinetti welcomed the three officers into his office, his face beaming.

"Come in, gentlemen, please. Make yourselves comfortable."

They moved their plastic chairs next to the psychiatrist's desk and waited in turn for him to sit down before taking their seats. Hal spoke first.

"Captain Roland told us to come so that you could tell us about Nico's problem and what we can do to help him."

Marinetti took a good look at them, one by one, as if he were trying to evaluate their personalities and their possible reactions to the news he was about to give them. His conclusion must have been positive because he stated bluntly:

"Lieutenant Andrade is going to have a baby."

Bewilderment lasted but a few seconds. Immediately the three of them burst out laughing and slapping their thighs, their eyes watering.

Marinetti looked at them baffled.

"If you find that funny . . ."

"So, what kind of a problem is that? If you think Nico will lose any sleep over getting a Xhroll pregnant . . ." Diego was choking with laughter as he tried to articulate the words.

"Nico is a son of a bitch, doctor," continued Igor, trying to calm down. "I'm sorry. I mean his moral scruples are really sort of . . ." Another burst of laughter cut off his words.

Marinetti cleared his throat before speaking again.

"Pardon me. Maybe I didn't make myself clear."

Everyone looked at him, teary-eyed with laughter.

"It's not the alien woman who is pregnant, gentlemen. It's your friend. Lieutenant Andrade is."

"He's pregnant?"

Diego's squeaky voice, half way between laughing and crying, triggered another fit, but of a different nature now.

"Does he know?" asked Hal in a very low voice, as if afraid Nico could hear them.

The psychiatrist nodded.

"I told him myself. A few hours ago."

There was a long silence.

"And how did he take it?" asked Igor.

Marinetti sighed.

"Badly. Very badly. At first he even assaulted me. But it's a natural reaction, of course. He didn't want to believe it. Then he started crying. At the moment, he is locked in his room and doesn't want to see anyone just yet. We must let him get over it by himself; he will need us later."

"But let me get this straight, Doctor . . ." Igor was talking fast and in a low voice, as he did every time emotional tension ran high. "First of all, that's impossible. Nico isn't a woman. Second of all, if we admit the impossible, how can you be so sure? Third of all, Nico doesn't have to put up with the situation. I suppose there is a way to remove . . . whatever it is he has inside of him, right? Some kind of abortion, I mean."

He looked at his shipmates, hoping they'd confirm his reasoning. Both of them nodded their heads and looked in turn at the psychiatrist.

"I'll try to organize my answer neatly for you, Komarov. First of all, I'm aware that a pregnancy would be impossible if it were among humans, but since the woman—if that's indeed what she is—belongs to a different species, we have no recourse but to face facts. Second of all, we are so sure because we contacted the *Harrkh* to find a solution to Andrade's apparent illness, and once the Xhroll got us on the right track, we were able to verify it ourselves. Third of all, our medical team cannot remove that fetus because, I'll try to put it simply, we're talking about a being who, in the absence of a uterus to grow in, builds a net for itself that implicates almost every one of the host's vital organs and literally sets up a parasitic existence. At the stage of development it's in now, we'd have to surgically remove most of the lieutenant's liver, both his kidneys, the prostate, the spleen, more than half his stomach . . . do I need to go on? Clearly, you all can see it's simply impossible."

Another silence set in.

"But . . . but, Doctor. The Xhroll must know how to go about it, right? Just like our own doctors know how to perform an abortion."

"That's a more difficult question to answer, Wilson. I know the commander has mentioned the possibility of addressing the issue with the Xhroll, but it is medically possible they don't know how to do it either, when the parasite's host is a human body. They don't have any experience with us, you understand? Besides, if it were a female human maybe, just maybe, there would be a chance for the parasite to implant itself in the uterus, and by extracting the whole uterus we could get rid of the problem. But that's just not the case."

"Doctor." Diego's voice was cracking, as if he were on the brink of tears again. "You told us before that Nico was expecting a baby."

Marinetti nodded his head slowly.

"Why all of a sudden are you talking about the 'parasite'? Will it turn out to be some kind of monster?"

The psychiatrist grinned.

"*Alien*? The old movie?"

Diego blushed.

"You have nothing to be ashamed of, García. I like movies, too. But to answer your question . . . we don't know. We have no way of knowing, but there's no reason to think it would be much different from its parents."

"Then why don't you say 'the boy' or 'the girl'? I, for one, would feel better about it."

"It's a matter of personality." The psychiatrist made a gesture of helplessness. "I feel that for now, and until we know for sure how the situation evolves, it's better to talk about a 'parasite.' If we see the problem has no solution and that Lieutenant Andrade will be forced to carry it to term, then it might be better to start humanizing, personifying it."

"So then?"

"Pay him a visit, if he agrees. If not, keep trying until he does, but please, above all, don't laugh at him. There's nothing funny about this."

"No there isn't," said Igor as he stood up. "There really isn't."

Commander Kaminsky took his time looking at the faces of the people in Assembly Hall, at every high-ranking man and woman aboard the *Victoria* who, in normal circumstances, met only once a month to discuss routine matters, to reassure each other with the news that everything was running smoothly. Every face looked tense now.

What only two days ago had been the brunt of obscene jokes had suddenly become the most serious challenge ever facing humanity.

"Ladies and gentlemen, I am sorry to have to inform you that the situation is practically desperate because, if we don't find a solution soon, this incident will lead us into the first interplanetary war in our history.

"I'm going to quickly summarize the situation; I will then ask for your opinions about it, and I hope you realize I want answers.

"All of you, female and male colleagues, know how the crisis started; I won't waste time explaining it. Four weeks after lieutenant Andrade's first symptoms began I was forced to swallow my pride and contact the alien spaceship for information. My main concern at that time was that we were dealing with a virus that could trigger an epidemic. For better or worse, that wasn't the case, and all you female and male colleagues already know the answer we got from the Xhroll. Also public knowledge is the fact that our medical crew is unable to remove the parasite living inside lieutenant Andrade's body.

"The *Harrkh*, following orders from its home planet, is now heading back toward our station with the expectation that we will hand over Lieutenant Andrade to them and they will take him to Xhroll, where they intend to observe the parasite's growth until it comes to term.

"The Xhroll demand the lieutenant be handed over to them, since to them he is the 'mother of one of their planet's citizens.' They promise to return Andrade once he has . . . ahem! . . . given birth.

"As a matter of principle, our planet's Central Government is not prepared to surrender Andrade because it considers that a violation of the most basic right to protection that every female and male citizen of our planet is guaranteed. And we have no way of knowing what fate awaits Andrade once he is taken so far away from our sovereign territory. Add to this the fact that this parasite, or, accepting the Xhroll terminology, this 'daughter or son' or 'female or male citizen,' is fifty percent human, then our world has as much right to him or her as the Xhroll may have."

Kaminsky flipped through his papers for a few seconds.

"As far as a possible extraction or abortion, however you wish to call it, we have consulted the Xhroll on the matter and they answered that, even though they probably wouldn't know how to perform one without endangering lieutenant Andrade's life, they would be unwilling to do so under any circumstances. Their world has an extremely low birth rate and every life is precious. Besides, it is a unique case in history and they don't want to miss the chance to study it and, if it turns out to be feasible, even replicate it. Please note the arrogance. Any questions?"

Colonel Ortega raised her hand, was given permission to speak, and stood up.

"Assuming that we all agree we don't want to surrender Andrade, couldn't we argue that all rights over the future entity belong to planet Earth because the lieutenant didn't know what he was risking and had no opportunity to refuse to conceive?"

Kaminsky grimaced as if he'd just bitten a lemon.

"I'm afraid, Colonel, that is one of our weakest points."

There was a hum of bewilderment in the room.

The commander continued.

"The Xhroll have a recording, obtained through their translator and sent over to me, of the complete conversation between Lieutenant Andrade and the Xhroll during the time they spent together in private. The transcription I have shows the woman explicitly warning Andrade that she is not taking any contraceptive measures. Andrade disregarded that warning and resumed a sexual relationship that was putting himself in danger."

"But he didn't know he was endangering himself," a voice said.

"Which means that the lieutenant assumed it was she who was taking the risk of conceiving and this didn't seem to him to be important enough to desist," the commander finished his thought. "This fact obviously puts us in an embarrassing situation in regards to our own moral principles, and in an absolutely unfavorable position with respect to the Xhroll."

"As far as morals are concerned, the Xhroll don't look so good either, because the woman knew Andrade could become . . . could conceive," Colonel Aichinger chimed in.

"Incorrect, Otto. During the woman's interrogation, which has also been transcribed for me, she maintains that right in front of her Andrade took a pill she assumed to be a contraceptive and he assured her that everything was in order."

"A contraceptive pill?" Several incredulous sounding voices were heard.

Kaminsky looked out for the chief medical officer, who had been invited to the meeting as a consultant.

"Doctor?"

Captain Roland cleared his throat and stood up.

"Lieutenant Andrade took an aspirin. He confessed it to me only a few minutes ago."

A hum of horror went around the room.

"Then the son of a dog tried to deliberately trick that woman without a thought of what could happen to her," Diana Ortega remarked, louder than she would have wanted.

"That's exactly right, Ortega." Kaminsky's voice was calm but his expression was angry. "The son of whomever behaved like a despicable pig with the first extraterrestrial beings we humans have come in contact with in our entire history. And right now a whole world is in conflict on account of that archaic alpha-male mentality we thought had ceased to exist after so many centuries fighting for gender equality." He paused and looked at them again with eyes like two dark wells. "I assure you I'd have no qualms about giving up Andrade if it weren't for the fact that it could signal our readiness to accept the Xhroll's wishes unconditionally."

"And what's his opinion on the matter?" asked another person in the room.

"Andrade?" The contempt in Kaminsky's voice was fierce. "At times he weeps like an old-fashioned damsel, at other times he rams into things like an angry bull. Two days ago he decided to stop eating, so we're feeding him intravenously. He says he'd rather slash his wrists than give himself up to the Xhroll. A very heroic stance, as you can see."

If any of the people there disagreed with the commander's words, they carefully refrained from expressing themselves. Everyone's eyes remained discreetly fixed on the table's polished surface, and when the silence became too noticeable, people's eyes continued their journey over the walls and toward the ceiling until they had no recourse but to descend from on high and resettle on Kaminsky's harder-than-ever face.

"What does the Central Government suggest?" asked the external equipment manager in a deliberately neutral voice.

"The Central Government allows us the privilege of making the first suggestion, since we all, female and male, have more data at our disposal."

"Which means," Ortega spoke up again, apparently to herself but loudly enough so that everyone heard. "Since we, female and male, are the ones who fucked up, we are hereby named planet Earth's female and male scapegoats. An honorary title, naturally."

"I didn't hear that comment, Colonel Ortega," said Kaminsky drily. "Don't let that happen again."

"Yes, sir." Ortega lowered her gaze, trying her best to stop interfering.

"You have two hours to present a list of viable proposals to me. No excuses. No delays. Two hours. In case you haven't heard the news, let me inform you that the *Harrkh*, like all Xhroll cargo ships, is equipped with weapons that could leave this station out of commission in a matter of minutes. That would be a provocation that would lead our planet to war, but let me be clear, neither you nor I would have to worry about any of that. Two hours."

Kaminsky picked up his papers and left Assembly Hall as the other occupants looked on in shock.

Nico was curled up in his bed in a dark sickbay room. He didn't know how long he'd been there and didn't care. Time was no longer measured by a clock but by the beatings of his belly. A constant, opaque beat pulsating warmly across his body, sometimes settling on his temples, at other times on his hands or throat.

If he lay still, curled up as he was now, its strength would decrease to an almost negligible level, but he always knew deep inside it was still there, signaling the growth of whatever it was that monster had planted inside of him.

He felt like crying again but fought the urge by clenching his fists and closing his eyes tightly. He'd cried enough already, made himself look foolish enough to himself and to others, the few who'd come in contact with him since they'd brought him to the hospital.

He had refused to see Diego and the others. He couldn't stand the idea of them teasing him, of their punny jokes, not to mention their pity or sympathy. He was Lieutenant Nicodemo Andrade, a red-blooded male, a man born to repair robots and seduce women despite how equal they were before the law. It just wasn't possible; what was happening to him just couldn't be possible. It must be a nightmare. That was the only explanation.

And yet he knew it wasn't. He knew it but was too much of a coward to admit it to himself and accept it. Or maybe it wasn't a matter of cowardice but of compassion. Compassion, pure and simple. What man wouldn't be horrified at the thought of what was happening inside of him?

Was that what a woman felt when she knew she had a son or daughter growing inside of her? Was it possible that every woman in the world had felt this frightened when she realized there was no turning back? It couldn't be. The human race would have become extinct centuries ago if women had felt the panic that was waking him up in the middle of the night drenched in sweat. But of course, that's what women were made for. They were happy when it happened to them. Weren't they? Or were the women of this century happy because they made the decision for themselves? How did the women of past centuries feel when their condition was the result of rape, as had just happened to him?

He pushed that thought aside immediately. He hadn't been raped. He had seduced that Xhroll. He'd been the first male human to have sex with an alien. He hadn't been raped. The pain he'd felt wasn't forced on him. It was a normal part of the Xhroll's erotic practices, a sign of the passion he'd unleashed in that woman.

The other thing had been an accident, an accident he couldn't have prevented. Or had it happened on purpose? No. That was crazy. It couldn't have.

At fifteen, in his small town, he had made his first girlfriend pregnant. She was slightly older than him and people said that he'd done it on purpose because the girl's family had money. But it wasn't true. It had been a mistake, the result of inexperience, just like now. The difference was that now it was he who had to suffer the consequences of their blunder. But that girl was able to go to a clinic to get an abortion and years later, when he came back from the military academy, they became friends again, even lovers.

Could he become friends with the Xhroll someday, or even go to bed with her again?

The thought gave him the chills. Somewhere on the *Victoria*, probably in Assembly Hall, his future was being decided.

Kaminsky, venomously cold as he was, would be trying to convince the High Command that the best solution would be to hand him over to the Xhroll and forget him. A token gift of goodwill for their extraterrestrial friends. No way! He'd kill himself somehow before that happened, by banging his head against the wall if he had to.

He pictured himself in a Xhroll hospital, surrounded by Xhroll doctors with their perfect, empty faces and he began to cry slowly, in spite of himself, fighting the tears that were now flowing unwillingly, his head under the pillow to better smother his sobs.

"Five minutes of your time, Colonel?"

Diana Ortega, eyes red and sweat drenching her hair, turned toward the voice on her right just as she placed her hand on her cubicle door after completing an uninterrupted thirteen-hour session. She was about to tell whoever it was to go to hell when she realized it was García, Andrade's friend. He didn't look like he'd slept a lot during the last few weeks, either.

"What's up, García? But tell me quick, before I fall asleep right here."

"Has a decision been made, Colonel?"

Ortega ran her fingers through her damp hair and let out a sigh.

"They're going to surrender him."

"Those sons of bitches!"

"García!" Her reaction was unconscious, and when she realized he was justified, she backed off right away. "Sorry. You're right. Whoever gave birth to Kaminsky must have been a man in disguise."

Diego looked like he'd just been hit below the belt.

"Again, I'm sorry. That was a real stupid comment, given the circumstances. This is not my day."

"So they're going to surrender him? Is the decision final?"

She nodded.

"If it's any consolation, they've managed to come to an agreement with those . . . Xhroll and allow another human to accompany him."

"Are they accepting volunteers?"

Ortega smiled and was tempted to kiss him to thank him for the loyalty his offer meant. Naturally she didn't.

"Don't get your hopes up, lieutenant. The Central Government has already appointed an escort."

"Who is it?"

"Charlie Fonseca."

Diego looked baffled.

"I don't know him. I could swear Nico doesn't either."

"A sort of liaison officer. No one knows quite what that role is on board the *Victoria*, something like a chaplain. Walks around and drafts reports, nothing out of the ordinary."

"And why him?"

"Nothing better to do, I suppose. How should I know? Go to sleep, García!"

Diana Ortega opened the door to her room, and a second before closing it behind her, she stuck her head back out and said:

"Oh! And it's not him, it's her."

Nico entered the commander's office feeling like his legs had turned to jelly. No one had said a thing to him, but they had shaved him, left his dress uniform laying on his bed, and accompanied him to the office with the same solemn expression one has when escorting an innocent man to the gallows.

As Nico came in, a quick look around told him the entire High Command was present; Kaminsky had decided he would spare him no humiliation.

He'd sworn to himself he'd be strong and honor his tough guy reputation, but for a moment he had the impression the office was tilting dangerously and he reached out his hand to grab anything that might stop him from falling. Someone quickly brought him a chair and it took a superhuman effort to turn it down.

"Lieutenant Andrade."

The sound of Kaminsky's voice was as painful as a fingernail scratching a chalkboard.

"Yes, sir."

He tried to crack a smile as a defense against the fear that gripped his throat when he met Kaminsky's eyes. It was a pathetic attempt, but he kept up the effort, tried to stop thinking.

"In thirty minutes you'll be boarding the Xhroll ship that will take you to our extraterrestrial allies' home planet. Earth's Central Government considers this to be the best solution and, if that wasn't clear enough, it's an order." He paused, in a way Nico thought to be full of malice. "You will stay with the Xhroll as a guest as long as necessary and, after that time, you will be returned to our planet and awarded substantial pension benefits for the rest of your life. Captain Charlie Fonseca will accompany you during your stay. I don't need to remind you that, because she is your ranking officer, you are under her authority, which is also that of the Earth Central Government."

He stood up.

"Lieutenant Andrade, personally and on behalf of our world, I wish you the best as you embark on this adventure. Don't forget, you represent our world to the Xhroll, and the eyes of every human woman and man are upon you. Have a good trip!"

Everyone in the room burst into applause and Nico, about to faint, felt an arm around his waist holding him so that he could use his right hand to salute. Infinitely grateful, he shifted his eyes for a moment and met another pair of eyes, brown like his, in a woman's face, and a smile similar to the one he used to sport in former times.

JOURNEY

The scrap of darkness that served as the door to the tiny cubicle they'd been assigned on the Xhroll ship vanished for a few seconds to admit Captain Fonseca, who showed up with two bottles in hand. Nico sat up on his elbow and watched as she approached with that springy stride characteristic of every brown person he'd ever known. Fonseca's skin was the only brown thing about her, though: her hair was much lighter, almost blonde, and her features were a mix that called to mind just about every race on Earth, recombined over generations to form a jigsaw that wasn't unpleasant to look at but wasn't especially memorable, either. Charlie Fonseca was such a completely nondescript woman that people only noticed her when she walked or smiled, and that was probably only because she was the sole human female in several billion kilometers.

"All set," she said happily. "No problem with us getting adjoining cubicles. I told them that we humans consider some minimal amount of privacy essential to our mental health and they seemed to get it right away. They wanted to assign you some kind of 'forever servant,' that's what it sounded like to me, but I convinced them to station one outside the door, not inside.

That way, if you ever need anything, all you have to do is give a shout and the Xhroll will be at your command."

"And what about you?" Nico asked, accepting the bottle Fonseca offered.

"I'll always be nearby, but don't get your hopes up, I'm not here to babysit you."

Nico pressed his forehead with his free hand.

"Headache?" she asked.

"I dunno. I feel groggy. I can barely remember leaving the *Victoria*. I remember like in a dream people clapping and wanting to shake my hand . . . a ton of Xhroll in a huge hall . . . dark, narrow aisles. Is all that true?"

She nodded, smiling.

"Just about everyone on board the *Victoria* gave me a letter or note for you; they sure seem to like you, Andrade. I left them over there, on top of your backpack, so you can read them when you feel like it. What you said you saw of the Xhroll is true. They even delivered a full-blown speech for us: some six or seven sentences."

The start of a laugh hung in the air.

"Sorry, Captain," said Nico, out of the blue.

"Sorry for what?"

He made a circular gesture.

"This. All this. And that you got stuck in the middle of it through no fault of your own."

She smiled again.

"I wouldn't have missed it for the world, Lieutenant. I was bored off my ass on the *Victoria*. Do you realize we're going to be the first to visit a planet inhabited by aliens?"

There was a pause.

"Under other circumstances, I'd be jumping for joy," he said at last.

"And under these, no?"

"Don't you know what I'm going through?"

"Sure I do. It's impossible not to."

"What, can you tell already?" Nico raised a hand to his belly, alarmed.

"Not yet, man, though you'd better start getting used to the idea that sooner or later you won't be able to wear your uniform pants; in a few months, they won't fit."

Nico turned his head toward the wall, trying to hide his eyes.

"It looks like the one who doesn't understand what's going on is you," Fonseca continued, unperturbed. "You have the rare privilege of being not just the first human to have sex with a member of an alien species, but the first man in our history to experience a real pregnancy. To be honest, I'm pretty jealous."

She drank down the rest of the bottle and threw it out the dark hole in the back wall.

"Ok, I'm going out for a stroll and let you rest a little. Starting now, we're going to lead a pretty routine but well-organized life. The Xhroll are designing you a nutrition program tailored to both needs, and by 'both' I don't mean you and me. You'll have daily gym sessions and language lessons, plus something like maternity classes. You'll also have to keep a diary and get medical checkups twice a day. In your spare time, which won't be much, you can do whatever you want, like on the *Victoria*. Well, not exactly like on the *Victoria*, considering what they say your main pastime used to be," she added with a sly grin. "If you need me for anything or feel like chatting, you can call me, I'm in the room next door. If you don't feel up to it, no worries, I won't bother you. Got it?"

He nodded, suddenly feeling overwhelmed. Charlie Fonseca crossed the dark room and left.

They didn't see much of each other over the next three or four days, counting "day" as every time they got woken up for the start of a shift. Nico showed up regularly for appointments, and Charlie came by his room with something to drink shortly before withdrawing for the rest period that loosely corresponded to Earth's night. The Xhroll behaved as always: with an infinitely reserved courtesy that, in Nico's case and to his surprise, started to feel like deference.

From the moment they'd set foot on the *Harrkh*, Nico hadn't seen *the* female or any other member of her sex; every one of his classes, trainings, and checkups had been carried out by male personnel only.

"Captain, ma'am, doesn't it seem strange that there are no women on board?" Nico asked Charlie one day as soon as she sat down.

"I think I might have seen one or two around. The commander must have ordered them to stay away from you. Probably due to your reputation as a lady-killer."

"Don't kid me, Captain. I'm not in the mood for jokes."

"Well truth be told, you're being insufferable, Andrade. If I weren't so multi-talented and easygoing and the *Harrkh* such a goldmine of mysteries, I'd be bored stiff being your escort. They told me you were a great guy, enterprising, witty, fun . . . and now it turns out you're becoming an old crybaby."

Nico pursed his lips and looked away. He, too, felt disgusted by the change taking place inside of him, but he didn't know how to stop it. Never in his life had he felt so stupid, so bitter, so passive as he had since this whole thing had begun.

The captain took an electronic game from her jumpsuit pocket and started adjusting the playing speed to maximum.

"What do you think of me, Captain?" Nico suddenly asked.

Fonseca raised her eyes and for an instant fixed them on the lieutenant's.

"I just told you."

"No, really. I'd like to know what you think of me overall."

Charlie switched off the device, put it back in her pocket, and leaned back in her chair.

"The truth?"

He nodded.

"Practically nothing. I need more data. But, ok: based on your history and what I've heard about you, I find you mildly amusing but fundamentally contemptible."

Nico couldn't help a slight gesture of surprise. Charlie continued as if she hadn't noticed.

"You strike me as a kind of *homo erectus* who, through some quirk of fate, was born in the twenty-third century and has some value as a museum piece, but that's about it. I find you weak, spineless, and dishonest. A man who doesn't love or respect anything except maybe himself, and that's only true of the love part, not the respect. A man who's used to winning but only because he never risks anything, he plays with marked cards. And the one time things go haywire, he thinks he has the right to a whole planet's sympathy, two planets', actually, and everyone should pat him on the shoulder and promise to fix everything without bruising his ego. Have I answered your question? Is that what you wanted to hear?"

He shook his head.

"That's not what I wanted to hear. But you've answered me, that's for sure."

Charlie stood up.

"Well, I'm leaving. I've already said too much."

Nico also rose.

"No, captain, don't go. I have another question. If that's what you think of me, why did you come?"

"Because, same as you, I'm an officer of the Central Government Fleet of the planet Earth, and I have my orders. I'm not here because of your beautiful dark eyes or because I'm that interested in xenology, though that's actually the best part of the trip. I had no choice, just like you, but I'm not complaining."

"Of course you're not complaining! You don't have a monster inside you!"

"I didn't insist on screwing a monster, either, if that's what you insist on calling the Xhroll, nor did I take an aspirin, thinking that way any possible problems would be the other person's. You're getting old enough to deal with the consequences of your actions, Andrade."

"I'm not a woman, dammit!"

She looked him up and down, slowly.

"No, lieutenant. You're not a woman. We're stronger."

"I am not a woman!" Nico shouted hysterically.

"Well, you better start learning how to be one, because you're not getting out of this with one of your smiles or snide, macho remarks. You're going to have to go through it all, and I guarantee you it won't be easy, just like it hasn't been easy for us women for the last fifty thousand years. You're going to learn a lot, Andrade, so you'd better stop getting all cocky on me because right now I'm all that you have. Me and what's inside you."

She turned and went through the door without so much as a "good night."

Nico stood in the middle of the room, his fists clenched in anger, waves of frustration coursing through his body.

Who did that idiot think she was, that butt-ugly fool who'd had to enlist in the Fleet just to feel like she mattered! He would never speak to her again. If the Central Government insisted that Captain Fonseca accompany him, fine, there was no way he could refuse, but it didn't mean they had to get along. There was no reason they had to have relations of any kind. From now on he'd only interact with the Xhroll, who at least seemed to respect him.

What he wouldn't give for a heavy wooden door to slam right now so Fonseca would know what he'd just resolved! But since there was no door or any heavy objects to hurl, he made do with punching himself in the belly as hard as he could.

Doubled over and calling himself an idiot over and over again, he fell onto his bunk and closed his eyes. After what seemed like forever, he fell asleep.

Charlie Fonseca stretched out on her bunk with her arms crossed comfortably under her neck and her gaze lost in the ceiling. She knew she wouldn't be able to sleep but it didn't really bother her; she'd never needed much sleep, never more than the required four hours when she was at the Academy. Now, with very little to do, her body was so far under normal exertion levels that time hung heavy. Mental fatigue was something else, though. Spending her days learning to speak Xhroll and trying to understand so many things, with nothing familiar to cling to for rest from time to time, was exhausting her brain. That's why she felt the need to retreat to solitude every three or four hours, to think about her own stuff in her own language without even trying to sleep. And the eight hours of nightly rest that the Xhroll needed, or believed that humans needed, were too much, even after logging her journal entries and reports, reviewing the day's lessons, and doing her physical exercises.

Done with all that, she fell into bed and lay thinking about Andrade. That poor idiot sure was screwed. But maybe no worse than some Mediterranean woman kidnapped by a Viking pirate and forced to live and give birth in some Norwegian village. The slight difference—and Andrade was right about this—was that he wasn't a woman. A lot of progress had been made in terms of equal rights and opportunities for the sexes but still, in spite of all the psychologists, anthropologists, and other "-ologists" in the world, males and females still thought and felt differently, and one thing both sexes understood very clearly was that males could not accidentally conceive. A mature embryo could be implanted in an artificial placenta and be carried to term, that had been done some half-dozen times, but those had always been lab trials with volunteer subjects who identified as female, whether or not they had a uterus. No person identifying as male had presented himself, and in the end, that line of research had been abandoned, though the possibility remained open. The procedure worked. If any male wanted to get pregnant, he had the legal right to. That was enough.

What hadn't occurred to anyone was that a human male could find himself in the situation that had been the sad norm for the planet's women for thousands of years: having to carry to term an unwanted pregnancy without even the comfort of a partner's support. That might explain the insurmountable divide between men and women, thought Charlie. The fact that for thousands of years men had been able to avoid their responsibilities while women, who might have done that too if they could, found themselves trapped by their own bodies, bodies that went on with the business of reproduction without asking their permission.

Whatever. She wasn't Andrade's partner or anyone else's. She could give him some degree of moral support but only if he was willing to accept it. As for everything else, her orders were clear enough.

Andrade would snub her for a while, which would let him reassert his independence. Later on they'd be fine. There really was no big hurry, they still had six or seven Earth months to go, provided the fetus developed normally. In two to three weeks they would land on Xhroll, and after that who knew what awaited them.

She could feel her eyes starting to close and let herself be carried away by drowsiness. One second later, a whistle near her head announced a visitor. She entered the door code and sat on the bed, trying not to show her surprise. This wasn't the reaction she'd expected from Andrade. She had assumed he'd be in his quarters kicking the wall or pounding his pillow with his fists, and yet he'd swallowed his pride . . . to do what? Ask her forgiveness? Not even as a joke. Insult her? Maybe, but not likely. Then, what?

The tall figure of a Xhroll took shape against the black haze of the doorway and Fonseca stood up. It wasn't Andrade. It was a woman with pale skin and light green eyes, who entered the cubicle without uttering a word. Charlie had to remember that a Xhroll doesn't think it necessary to say things twice: if by opening the door you're giving them permission to enter, there's no need to use a phrase like "May I come in?" or "Excuse me" or any other such human silliness. So the Xhroll stood in front of her, and Charlie, as always, felt like any second now one of her hands would seize the Xhroll's chin of its own accord and peel off the rubber mask to reveal the true face underneath. Naturally, that did not happen.

"I want to speak with you," the woman said.

Charlie sat down on her bed but stood up again because, in spite of all her gestured invitations to sit, the Xhroll remained standing.

"I implanted in the Earth abba."

Charlie blinked slightly, like she always did when she didn't quite get something.

"I want to know your legal and emotional status. Do you have legal rights over the terrestrial? How do you share with him?"

"Do you mean are we married or something? Are we a couple? No. Absolutely not. Our being of different sexes is sheer coincidence. My government has sent me to escort and observe him, but I have zero emotional relationship with Andrade and my rights over him are purely hierarchical: I'm a captain and he's a lieutenant. I'm his superior officer, that's all. I thought you all knew that already."

"You have no authority over his private decisions?"

Charlie thought it over.

"If they're strictly private, no. Only if they somehow affect humanity or the Fleet. Why? What's going on?"

"Nothing that affects humanity or the Fleet. I need no more answers."

"But I do." Charlie's tone would have signaled to a human that she was about to get angry; the alien did not register it.

"Ask," she said.

Charlie began to feel like she was in one of those ancient legends where a knight-errant's life depends on riddling with a sphynx.

"Is what you're going to ask Andrade strictly private?"

"Yes."

"Can you tell me what it is?"

"You have no authority to know if he does not choose to tell you."

"If it's something that affects his legal status, he can't make any decisions without my consent."

Charlie was answering instinctively without knowing what the Xhroll was getting at, but this was exactly the wrong moment in the two species' relationship to let Andrade make any decision without first consulting her.

"I want to ask him to accept my . . .," the automatic translator seemed to hesitate for a few seconds, ". . . protection on Xhroll."

"Protection? Is there some kind of danger?"

"The unborn was implanted by me. It is my privilege, if no previously established right exists."

Charlie's brain was working at full speed.

"What does the legal right of, uh, protection consist of?"

"I will share with him . . ." The translator was silent for almost a full minute and only the Xhroll's words, spoken in her native language, filled the cubicle. "There is no translation for everything I am trying to explain. Our linguists have only found equivalent concepts for superficial cultural exchanges. We did not think the opportunity would come so soon to communicate our deeper frameworks with strangers."

"Are you talking about marrying him?"

The translator seemed to stammer and fall silent. The Xhroll also paused for a few seconds.

"Possibly," she finally answered. "I lack sufficient information. Are you willing to work on the database with me to reach a better understanding?"

"I'm willing as long as the information is reciprocal. I can't make any decisions without knowing all the factors."

"I agree. We Xhroll also think that way."

"Then I'll see you tomorrow. Where?"

"I will come get you at the end of your rest period."

Once she'd said what she came to say, the Xhroll left the cubicle without saying goodbye, something Charlie still couldn't get used to. Still, other than the Xhroll language apparently having no courtesy phrases, no ways to express wishes, or anything usable for light conversation, it actually wasn't as hard to understand them as it was with some humans. At least they spoke their minds. In any case, the chance to elicit more information about their respective cultures was more than she'd hoped for and dovetailed nicely with her orders. Even better, the idea had come from the Xhroll; humans could never be accused of trying to worm their way into their hosts' private affairs.

Charlie turned off the light and went to sleep, willing the remaining four hours to pass quickly so she could start better understanding the Xhroll.

What woke him was a dull pain in his groin, coupled with an urgent need to urinate. He stumbled to his feet, searching in the dark for the corner the Xhroll had set up as a bathroom. He stopped before he got there, because something wet and warm was sliding down his legs.

Holy motherfucker! he thought. *Now all of a sudden I can't hold it!*

The pain was getting stronger and he was starting to feel a tightness in his chest. The room's darkness turned oppressive, threatening. He took a few steps toward the bed to turn the light on when he felt another wave of liquid spilling downward. That's when he realized his bladder hadn't played a trick on him, he was hemorrhaging and he must be hemorrhaging in a big way to have mistaken it for a stream of urine. Something was very wrong with his insides, that much was clear.

Huddled on the floor, holding his belly with both hands, he started to call out for his captain like a soldier wounded in battle. But then he pictured Charlie Fonseca smiling scornfully, calling him an old crybaby, and with effort he switched languages and started yelling the Xhroll words they'd taught him to say if he ever needed immediate help.

One second later, the lights went on and the Xhroll assigned to him burst into the room, lifted him off the floor, laid him on the bed, and went out into the hall to sound the alarm. There was blood everywhere, blood so thick and red that he felt sick. A sticky heat made him close his eyes, trying to control his distress.

When he opened them again, he was lying on some kind of elevated slab surrounded by impassive Xhroll who moved quickly around him like in one of his recurring nightmares.

Now I'm going to die, he thought. *They've been fooling me to make me cooperate. The monster's ready and it's going to tear me open to get out. They knew all along this would happen. They knew it.*

He tried to shout again, calling for the captain, but he couldn't. Someone held an icy instrument against his face. He fought to free himself and could feel his strength failing, his self-awareness slipping away until a point came when he stopped caring about anything.

When he woke up, Charlie Fonseca sat next to him typing into a small electronic device that looked like something left to her by an old ancestor. She looked up, smiled, and kept working a few seconds longer. Then she disconnected the device, stuck it in her pocket, and smiled at him again.

"You're one tough nut, Andrade."

He stretched out on the bed feeling weak but pleasantly numb, almost happy. He was pain-free and, by the looks of it, had survived.

"Am I ok?" he asked.

"Right as artificial rain. Both of you."

He frowned and looked away.

"I don't mean to be cruel, Lieutenant, but it seemed best to tell you before you started getting your hopes up. Apparently, what happened was like your body's try at rejection or spontaneous abortion. But she or he won. I'm sorry, for your sake."

Nico didn't answer. He passed his hand over a stomach that was already starting to curve, even when lying down. His hand curled into a claw near his belly button; Charlie covered his hand with hers and, very gently, lifted it away from his body and rested it next to him on the bed.

"It won't do any good to beat yourself up, Andrade. Fetuses will fight to live, you know." She didn't expect him to say anything. "Speaking of which, why don't we give it a temporary name? So we don't have to always say 'the fetus,' which sounds terrible, or 'he or she,' which, just between us, always sounded super clunky to me, not to mention stupid."

"I've never been very creative when it comes to names. Besides, I couldn't care less what it's called, I'm not going to keep it."

"So, what are you planning to do? Leave your son or daughter on Xhroll, as if it weren't a human being at all?"

"It's not my son or daughter." Nico was starting to feel that impotent rage again, the sort of rage that had become part of him in a few short months. "It's like some kind of tumor. No one keeps a tumor when the doctors know how to remove it."

"Calm down, Andrade. No one can force you to keep it. The Central Government will find the right guardian for it."

"You, for example?"

She made a face he couldn't quite read before it turned into a smile.

"No, lieutenant, I don't think so. I told you once before that I'm not cut out to be a nanny. You want something to drink?"

He nodded, and Charlie went to find one of the usual bottles.

"You're not upset because I didn't call you last night when I was bleeding?"

Charlie seemed genuinely surprised.

"No. Why? Everyone's free to die in whatever company they prefer and it's pretty clear you and I haven't really hit it off. Besides, it wasn't last night. It was two weeks ago, and in two weeks I can get over anything."

"Two weeks?" Nico's voice sounded shocked.

"Take it easy. You've saved yourself two weeks of boredom. We're just about to reach Xhroll."

Nico swallowed.

"And when we get there?"

She sighed and rubbed the back of her neck.

"That's just what I wanted to talk to you about. That's why I'm on guard duty here like an idiot, so they don't come asking you to make decisions before you and I have reached an agreement."

"What kind of agreement?" Nico started to sit up in bed, but he couldn't quite manage it until he accepted the captain's arm.

"If you were standing up I'd tell you to sit down, Lieutenant, because you're in for a pretty big shock. To be honest, it's taken a while for me to come around to the idea myself, and I have plenty of imagination."

"Tell me." Nico's mouth had suddenly gone dry.

"Lieutenant Nicodemo Andrade, will you marry me?"

Nico was confused for an instant, but just for an instant. Two seconds later he was laughing so hard the bed shook.

Charlie waited for the first fit of laughter to subside.

"This is serious, Andrade. For two weeks I've been exchanging information about social structures with these people and right now the one thing that's clear, and I swear the whole thing is fucking complicated, is that in your present circumstances you are no longer an ordinary individual. You've become an 'abba,' someone able to carry a life inside you. In other words, a mother. Don't interrupt me, Lieutenant! To continue: abbas merit respect, deference, practically devotion from the rest of society, but they have almost no civil rights because they become something like public property, a type of shared asset that must be preserved and protected. An abba has to be protected by a full citizen, who might be the one who engendered the baby or might just be any member of that class of beings who are capable of impregnating someone and who are called 'ari-arkhj.' In your case it was the blonde, green-eyed female, and she's prepared to take on the role of ari-arkhj. Speaking in human terms, it's like she's prepared to marry you and put you under her protection. You can turn her down, of course, but then a perfect stranger will take charge of you, someone high up in the Xhroll hierarchy. I don't know if I've mentioned it, but they are a pathetically hierarchical people. Compared with them our Fleet, even the special units, are like kindergarteners."

"If you don't belong to anyone by the time we land, you'll belong to whoever's highest up on the ladder. I don't know who that might be, nor do I care just now."

"But that's outrageous! It's totally humiliating!" Nico's eyes were wide with fear and anger.

"Shut up and let me finish! Any second now a Xhroll's going to come in and we won't be able to talk privately."

Nico shut up.

"Good. Where was I? Oh yeah. It seems that because of, or in spite of, their sense of hierarchy, they respect laws above all else, so if you already belong to someone by the time we land, the Big Cheese will have to accept the situation, like it or not."

"Meaning," said Nico in a lugubrious voice, "better the devil you know."

"Exactly."

Nico lay down again and closed his eyes.

"Don't act crazy, Andrade. You have to decide, and fast."

"But what the hell do you want me to decide?"

Charlie grabbed him by his shirtfront and lifted him a few inches off the bed.

"Either you marry that Xhroll woman and me, or they'll turn you over to someone who's not only a complete stranger but an alien, too."

"And why do I have to marry you?"

She released him with an exasperated grunt.

"It's incredible that a moron like you managed to pass the Fleet's entrance exams! And even more incredible that a woman like me is trying to convince said moron to marry her," she muttered to herself.

"Are you going to explain, or what?"

"Listen, and listen good because I'm not going to say it again. If you only marry the female Xhroll, they have all rights over you and your daughter or son. If they decide you're not going back to Earth, for example, you'll never, ever go back. Of course that might trigger a war, but you won't care about that. We're not going to destroy an entire planet just to free you.

"The only way we humans will have any say in the matter is if you are legally bound to another human, ideally beforehand. Oh, I'm sure you'd rather marry one of those women who advertise natural fruit in the holos, but believe me, you're not what I had in mind for a husband either."

There was a long silence while Nico stared at his fingernails and Charlie, hands in her pockets, watched him staring at them.

"And how do you plan to manage the beforehand part?" he finally asked.

Charlie gave a sigh of relief.

"I've explained to them that on our world there's something called divorce, as well as temporary or permanent marriage. I admitted to them that we're temporarily married and that, because of your . . . pregnancy, I felt insulted and decided not to extend our contract. But the proof that our marriage is still valid is that I'm here. Our Government had no option but to send as your escort the only person with any legal rights over you; the fact that I'm your superior in the Fleet's hierarchy is a fortunate coincidence. Now all we have to do is ratify our marriage before witnesses for everything to be legally set."

"And they believed you?"

"Naturally they believed me. It's the honest truth." Charlie's eyes glanced furiously at the door, the walls, the ceiling, trying to make Nico understand that they could be listening in on them.

"Well, Captain, as long as the explanations they gave you are just as, um, 'straightforward,' then we're good."

Charlie had been acting as liaison officer for too many years not to know that Nico was right and that in all likelihood the Xhroll had only told her what suited their own ends. But she didn't think this was the best time to discuss the possible lack of truth in the Xhroll's statements.

"So, do you agree to stay married to me, Lieutenant Andrade?"

Nico's faint grin hinted at his smile from the good old days.

"Of course, Charlie. What choice do I have? As long as you're ready to tolerate a certain amount of self-denial. 'Cause for certain things, you're just not my type."

"I'll survive, Lieutenant." Her smile was merely a civilized way of showing her teeth. "I wouldn't sleep with you if you were the last stud on Earth."

Charlie considered the conversation over and, in Xhroll fashion, left the infirmary without saying another word.

XHROLL

THE DEAD
AND THE LIVING

They landed four days after the two marriage ceremonies took place and both events reflected the typical modus operandi of their alien hosts: speed, effectiveness, extreme simplicity.

Charlie and Nico were transported in a small windowless surface vehicle driven by the Xhroll woman whom they had decided to call Ankkhaia, knowing full well her real name sounded a far cry from that.

In their vehicle, the three passengers rolled or floated—the humans couldn't tell which—for about twenty-five minutes, stopped for a few seconds, and then, judging by the feeling in their stomachs, plunged down at top speed in some kind of elevator for about three minutes longer. Then the top section opened and the three found themselves in a room about the size of the *Victoria*'s exterior hangar. It must have been used as an arrival terminal since there were several more vehicles stationed nearby.

Feeling claustrophobic despite the room's dimensions, Charlie and Nico stepped out of the vehicle while Ankkhaia rushed to help her brand-new husband, ignoring his look of pure hatred.

From the beginning of the journey the two humans had speculated separately about what that far-away planet, the first inhabited world an earthling would come in contact with, would be like. Although both had envisioned many different possibilities, none fit with what they saw before them now: a simple hangar, apparently located underground, that could be located on Xhroll, on Earth, or on any old space station.

No reception committee awaited them, as if the fact of their being the first humans to visit the planet gave them no right to preferential treatment.

Ankkhaia stepped forward to meet another woman coming toward them riding some kind of floating chair, and shortly afterward, the translator's voice filled the hangar with Nico's furious screams as he was forced into a seat.

"We cannot take any risks with a xhri abba," the newcomer informed Charlie. "Explain it. The abba's own life and that of the hol'la are too important."

Nico kept yelling at the top of his lungs as he tried to unfasten the seat belt they'd used to buckle him in. It didn't seem to have any release buttons or clasps at all.

"Shut up! Stop acting like an idiot and do as they say. We are ambassadors from our planet and I won't let you make fools out of us," Charlie hissed at him. "That's an order."

Nico had been in the Fleet too long not to recognize an order when he heard it, so he stifled his protests, looked intently toward the end of the very long corridor and clenched his teeth.

For the thousandth time in the last few months he felt ridiculous and humiliated, a mere object without free will or the power to make his own decisions. He was someone to perform tests on, to be exercised and fed properly, a second-class being who did not get straight answers, a mere piece of swelling flesh.

He looked furiously at the three limber-legged women walking briskly next to him, their three flat bellies nice and empty, and felt like howling in despair.

Charlie gave a quick glance toward Nico's seat and looked away again so no one would spot her feeling so sorry for him. The situation was difficult enough for her; she was well trained and sound as a bell. So it must be particularly hard for him to have every one of his lifetime beliefs come crashing down! She hadn't told him anymore about what she'd learned about the Xhroll because she didn't think he could stand it. It was better for him to discover what was in store for him in stages. Maybe, as the pregnancy progressed, his own body chemistry would prepare him for the docile, passive role the alien culture assigned their abbas. If not, then she'd try to protect him, but she doubted she could do much to help because it was a matter of a whole planet's attitude toward a social phenomenon.

They went down an endless series of corridors, halls, and elevators, hardly coming across a soul. At last, Charlie dared ask why everything looked so empty.

"We have chosen this time for your arrival because it happens to be the rest period for most service personnel in this area. We do not want to overstimulate the abba. Once we have settled him in his rooms and left him under the care of the team responsible for him, you will be free to express your wishes as to how to spend your own time," answered the woman accompanying them.

"I'd like to take a look around the planet," said Nico.

The two Xhroll turned toward him with the absolute lack of emotion that made them so menacing.

"Abbas have no right to express any wish unless they do so through their ari-arkhjs," said the woman to Charlie. And looking at Ankkhaia added: "Didn't you explain it to them?"

Ankkhaia nodded.

"Our society is very different and though certain things have been explained to me in theory, I'm not used to putting them into practice. When I must react quickly I tend to do as I did back on Earth," cut in Charlie, trying to defuse the situation.

"You are not on Earth."

Nico felt that hysterical laughter that comes from nervous tension bubbling up, and bit the inside of his cheeks to stop it in its tracks.

"Back home every person answers for him or herself," Charlie insisted.

"The abba too?"

"Of course."

"That is a very negative custom. It is harmful to the group."

Charlie shrugged under the icy stare of the two Xhroll. She didn't feel like starting a debate about the benefits of having individuals speak for themselves and be responsible for their own actions. She was getting tired of the situation and the only thing she really wanted was to hand over Andrade to the team in charge of his care and take off for someplace she could be alone; given the choice, an open space where the air actually smelled like something, like anything but the odorless recycled air of the last few years. Luckily, her orders didn't entail constant surveillance and she could shrug off the task of acting as the guard, the babysitter, and now the voice of her lieutenant. *Some honeymoon!* The thought just popped into her head, and the idea made her burst out laughing so hard she had to mask it as a coughing fit.

The two Xhroll women stood there woodenly, as if stuck in place. Then they quickly abandoned Charlie in front of a white mist door, merely saying, "Possible risk to the abba's health," before pushing Andrade's chair through. He looked back at her with eyes dilated by fear until he disappeared into the mist. The women stepped in after him and vanished, but then Ankkhaia stuck her head back out.

"Wait for me here. I will settle the abba in properly. Then I will show you something of Xhroll."

If Nico heard the offer he must have felt tempted to kill them both, but the misty doors seemed to have good sound-proofing properties.

It is difficult to express oneself in human language. The structure is simple enough, yet the concepts are confusing, ambiguous. There are words with several meanings, and others whose meanings are so unclear they mean almost nothing. I know the problem is partly the lack of references or associations, my own ignorance about their world. My orders are to write down my observations using the xhri language to improve my understanding of the aliens. According to our linguists, thinking in their language is the only way for me to understand them and make them comprehensible to our people. But it's exhausting. Our most basic concepts don't align. I'm not sure I'll be able to carry out my assignment in a satisfactory manner.

They constantly use sex in their language. Everything must be either feminine or masculine, even inanimate objects. To refer to people, they must use both possibilities. When speaking in the first person one must choose between them. Humans always know which one to use, but it's hard for me. Am I a *he* or a *she*? The human says I am a woman and must use the feminine form to refer to myself. And yet, within their own sexual framework, the being able to implant life in another being is masculine and the one receiving it is feminine. That, to me, means I am a *he*. However, the two xhri agree that I am a *she*. I will have to decide what I'll use for myself and what I'll use to refer to the he-human and the she-human. They told me their names: Charlie and Nico. To them that's not important, naming another being. They call me Ankkhaia. They don't register the pain the Xhroll feel when given a name out of ignorance. They don't know one must not name what is not known. They don't understand the most obvious of things.

I showed Charlie a small part of our outside world, Xhroll's crust. She doesn't understand that we choose not to live outside, that we don't take advantage of (her words) the whole exterior space of our planet instead of living underground. She doesn't understand that we would damage the planet that's home to us and alter its balance, as happened some time ago. I didn't tell her that. We don't want them to know we were once capable of destroying what gave us life. And that we could do so again if we didn't exert a great deal of self-control.

According to Charlie, the xhri do the same thing with small areas of their world they call parks and nature reserves, but her people wouldn't accept a Xhroll-like solution. Their selfishness is wrong, but they don't understand that. I believe Charlie does understand and accepts it, although she finds it strange. The abba does not. She now calls us monsters and is sad most of the time. The doctors say it could be a xhri reaction to . . . gestation? Our abbas also lose their psychological balance on occasion, for body chemistry reasons.

It is sad that the abba is suffering and, for me, it is incomprehensible. Our abbas feel happy to have a life inside them, to be able to deliver a new being to Xhroll. But Nico is suffering. Charlie says Nico feels "humiliated." I don't understand the term. Charlie says it means to be forced to do something that is beneath one's dignity. I don't understand "dignity" either. But I do understand "forced," and what the abba is feeling is objectively not accurate.

When I shared with the abba my desire to conceive, she wanted it too. I followed my orders by warning her in case she didn't, but she took a fake pill and that meant, to me, that she agreed. I asked about it later, but Charlie never answers clearly. I know that something is being left unsaid; that's why I wait.

This is the second time I have an abba under my protection. That should make the situation easier, but that's not so. I've also tried to implant in a xhri from another world three times before, but it has never worked. That's why I feel happy now, for myself and for Xhroll. The abba doesn't want to see me, and calls me a monster. I'm spending with Charlie the time I would spend with the abba if I could.

This is a strange situation. I've never spent so much time with another ari-arkhj before. It's stimulating to my brain, but also exhausting. We share in a way that only an ari-arkhj and abba do. Charlie asks questions all the time and is smart, with a quick and curious mind, just like an arkhj's. Charlie also asks for help, just like an abba. Everything is mixed together in Charlie.

These people are incredible! They live in some god-awful place, a kind of gigantic, planet-sized space station, when they have a dream world on the surface. They spend their days stuck down here, with artificial lighting and recycled air, and only go up onto the crust, as they call it, during their free time or to work on maintenance and conservation of the natural world, which everyone in the community does, some part-time and many on a full-time basis. They're like their world's gardeners, like a twentieth-century homemaker cleaning and polishing the room they called the living room but that no one ever entered or used.

I'm really fed up. I've got the feeling they have no interest in showing me anything except the surface of their world and of their language, which seems simple at first glance; they say whatever they want to say and have a term to refer to each thing. And yet it's draining, I don't know why. Maybe it's precisely because humans always try to complete the message with stuff that isn't found in language and that, for the Xhroll, simply doesn't exist: No tone, no body language, no meta-message, or any such trifles. They don't seem to have poetry, a sense of humor, or any of the things that make life bearable for us humans. They are beautiful, patient, courteous, efficient, cold. Frankly, they're disgusting, and it must be because they seem human, but they're not. If they looked differently, if they were flat-out alien, weird, monstrous, it would be much easier. You wouldn't constantly make the mistake of treating them as if they were work colleagues. If every time they opened their mouths I saw three rows of teeth oozing poison slime, it would be easier not to lose sight of the fact that we probably have nothing in common.

At times I swear I could kill that motherfucker Andrade for having brought me here. It turns out that after all our hopes and fears, there's nothing exotic about Xhroll, not on the inside, not on the outside. Although inside, to be honest, they've only allowed me to see hallways and public rooms. And true to their straightforward nature, they haven't even bothered to find a socially acceptable excuse; they've simply said things like: "We do not want you to go in there; it's an area we do not want a stranger to see." It's taken me weeks to get used to it.

Outside, Xhroll is like an improved version of Earth. Its nature is so natural it seems fake, as if they dust it clean every morning. It's wonderful to be able to take walks outside, of course, but I expected something else and so did our government.

Nico gets gloomier every day. I'm not sure if it's a matter of his own hormones or if they're administering some type of drug, but he doesn't show the slightest interest in anything I tell him and I can't get him to speculate about our hosts. "I wonder how their hierarchical structure works," I muse. "You already explained it to me on the ship." And I'm not about to tell him I made most of it up. "What do you think their weapons are like?" I persist. Shrug. "Have you spotted robots of any kind?" Shrug. "What about medical assistant robots?" Nod. Looks like he's even lost all professional interest in his surroundings.

I get bored and take off for the surface, the only place I'm always allowed to go by myself without special permission. I must find out what it is they need from us, what we could sell them, what we could be interested in buying. I've got to find out their approximate level of knowledge, but they refuse to talk about much of anything. They simply refuse. They don't need anything, they say. They want nothing. They've got nothing to offer.

And I don't believe that. I just can't.

Nico lay on a metal spider of sorts that exercised his muscles without him having to make any effort. Charlie roamed up and down the room, stumbling over her own words under the man's blank stare.

"How many more times do I have to tell you the same story so you get it, damn it! On a planet where they're becoming extinct as a species, do you think it's right to kill a guy under our very noses and no one, male or female, bats an eye?"

Nico shrugged.

"Do you think that's normal?" Charlie bellowed.

"I don't think anything they do is normal. But, as far as it goes, it's not so outlandish. Have you seen them show any emotion, ever?"

Charlie shook her head vehemently, as if trying to clear it by stirring it up.

"It's not that, no. It's not that they haven't shown any emotion; I expected that. It's the fact they simply called a . . . like a cleaning service team, some kind of high-end trash collectors. They picked the body up—you can imagine its state after falling more than 250 feet off a cliff—and everyone just went on with their work as if nothing had happened."

Charlie took a deep breath, put her hands in her pockets and stared at Nico as if waiting for an explanation. He looked at the ceiling and sighed.

"Just take it easy, girl. After all, they're not human males or females. And if you think about it, a body is just that: meat. Garbage. Trash. You should be thankful they haven't served it to us for lunch. What did you expect from the alien Valkyries?"

Charlie turned around and left without saying goodbye.

She was beginning to hate Andrade's sense of humor, his moustache, his big belly, and even his tone of voice for that matter.

She walked down the hallways, hands deep in her jumpsuit pockets, head shaking now and then as she tried to push away the image she kept seeing in her mind, that fall down the cliff, which couldn't have lasted longer than four or five seconds but felt eternal to her. She had kept screaming much longer after the Xhroll's own scream had ended, until she realized the yells came from her own throat only.

She couldn't get it out of her head: the Xhroll falling like a puppet, the scream in her throat, and a ridiculous, awful, frustrating burning sensation in her nose. Something inside told her it was disrespectful to scratch your nose while a human being (correction, a nonhuman being, but its equivalent) was about to smash onto the rocky valley floor. And the feeling that it just couldn't be, he couldn't just plunge down like that, in front of everyone, with no one doing anything to save him.

And then Charlie herself, one hand rubbing her nose, the other stretching toward Ankkhaia in an unconscious gesture of solidarity and comfort. The alien's clear, cold eyes empty of all feeling, the clean-up crew, fast, efficient, silent. The world was back in place, Ankkhaia was telling her about the history of their language, of the cultural revolution responsible for the new conflict-minimizing system that allowed for absolute clarity of intent and expression.

Charlie's mind recalled long-forgotten linguistics classes, the notion that an unambiguous language was impossible. She remembered the steady degradation, the automatization, the total closing down of feelings, and the thoughts that would cease to exist the moment they couldn't be named, but she felt unable to articulate any of it. Not when someone had just died right before her eyes, before half a dozen impassive Xhroll.

After a while Ankkhaia realized something was wrong.

"What's the matter, Charlie?"

"I'm not quite sure. I suppose I'm feeling a bit sad."

Ankkhaia merely looked at her.

"Because of what just happened," she added. In spite of herself, Charlie always found herself offering more explanations than she had intended when a Xhroll stared at her in silence for a few minutes. "One life less."

"No. Not for Xhroll."

"What do you mean? Do you have some type of religion? Does that Xhroll who just died have some kind of significance?"

"Life is an intimate subject for the Xhroll, Charlie. We do not want to share with strangers."

With that answer in mind, Charlie pressed her lips together and took the elevator that would take her to Xhroll's surface. She was dying to get out of there. Out of there for good.

Time went on, although every day felt the same as the next, there being no holidays or celebrations or anything to distinguish one day from any other. For Nico, Xhroll was the maternity ward at a maximum-security prison; for Charlie, the sprawling garden at a public mental hospital. Their relationship had become harmless, anodyne. Charlie visited him daily. They exchanged a few empty phrases, and after an hour had gone by, she was dying to leave his cell while he in turn closed his eyes, clearly showing he was grateful that she had stood up to leave.

The Xhroll kept being their polite, cold selves and were still refusing to let her meet anyone other than Ankkhaia. Ankkhaia was still her guide, her confidant, her teacher, her . . . friend? She was everything they had on that planet that seemed so natural and so incomprehensible at the same time. Some days Charlie woke up happy, in a good mood, willing to get things done and connect with someone, visually at least. On other days, however, she felt she had the weight of the whole planet on her shoulders and time was standing still. If it weren't for the fact that Nico's tests showed the baby was developing as expected, she would feel that time on Xhroll was a gummy resin or a honeyed glob. Something yellow, soft, and sticky that got a hold of you and didn't let you go.

By sheer willpower she got out of bed, because if there was anything in the world she didn't want to become, it was a lazy fat cat like Lieutenant Andrade. Today she was determined to try to get some kind, any kind of valid information from Ankkhaia. She had already given up on her priorities; any data, public or private, would do for her report. As soon as they got back home and the debriefing sessions began, every officer, male and female, newbie and oldie, would think she was trying to hide something. She gritted her teeth. Her stomach muscles were burning, but she just had to ignore it. Fifty sit-ups. Fifty, not one less. She put political considerations aside, cleared her mind, exhaled fully, and continued her crunches.

She wasn't even halfway through her workout routine when, for the first time since living on Xhroll, a bodiless voice echoed around her room repeating a message in a language that was incomprehensible to her.

For an instant she gasped, as if something had kicked her in the uterus. How was it possible that she couldn't understand that language? From the very start of her studies, it had been made clear that the Xhroll only had one language. It was absurd for them to have another language hidden up their sleeve, but even though very similar to the Xhroll she knew, whatever was playing through the loudspeakers sounded like a whole different tongue. It wasn't a dialect. Another stage of the language, perhaps? The Xhroll spoken on the planet centuries ago? Ridiculous. Who would start sending out messages in an obsolete tongue that only a couple of scholars would be able to understand?

She quickly put on one of the Xhroll jumpsuits she'd gotten used to wearing and dashed over to the closest message column. There was an exceptionally high number of messages, and it took her much longer than usual to make sure none were addressed to her.

Trying her best to enunciate her words clearly, she recorded a message for Ankkhaia: *Contact me as soon as possible. I need information.*

Then she returned to her cubicle. It had been an oasis of peace and privacy in the midst of Xhroll's uniform public sleeping quarters, but now it seemed like a small cell that made her stick out and cut her off from the others. She'd wait to hear from Ankkhaia, and if that took too long she'd go see Nico. She didn't know what was going on, but there were far fewer Xhroll than normal in the hallways, and in uncertain times it was best to stick together. She'd give Ankkhaia one hour, no more.

When the strange voice came through the loudspeakers, the Xhroll helping Nico settle into a transport recliner so he could be taken to his therapy session stiffened as he stood next to the bed, remaining completely still for the two or three minutes the announcement lasted. Then he asked Nico to get out of the recliner and back into bed.

"Why? What about today's session? Don't you care about my state of mind anymore? Is something unusual going on?"

"Your ari-arkhj will let you know when he comes to visit you."

"What's going on, goddammit?" bellowed Nico from his bed as the Xhroll put the recliner back in its place and started to exit the cubicle. "Have my ari-arkhj come here immediately! Please . . . I'm feeling very anxious," he added. Although it bothered him to play that role, he knew it was probably the only way to force a Xhroll nurse to look for Charlie or, failing that, the Valkyrie.

"Xhroll has lost a life, abba. The pain is intense."

Feeling just as perplexed about getting an answer for the first time in months as about the answer itself, Nico couldn't think of anything else to stop the Xhroll. He was still staring at the mist that had swallowed him when Charlie oozed into the room like an ectoplasm, head and shoulders first.

"Nico, something's wrong here. These motherfuckers are keeping something from us, besides having lied to us about teaching us their language."

"Hey, take it easy! And let's see if you can tone down that sexist language of yours. You women have a tendency to swear as soon as you get hysterical . . ."

"I'm not in the mood for jokes, Nico! The situation may be very serious. We have no idea what's going on; it could be an invasion, a war, an epidemic, anything! And they've left us sitting here without any explanation. I didn't even get a message from Ankkhaia. What are you laughing about?"

"About the fact that, for the first time on this damned trip, I know something you don't."

"Let's hear it."

"Someone died on them. I suppose they're going to the funeral or something."

Charlie stared at Nico, stone cold sober.

"Are you a moron or something?"

"No, it's exactly what the male nurse who was supposed to take me to the interrogation session, and didn't, just told me."

"But that's silly! Not that long ago that guy killed himself right in front of all of us and it was business as usual. And now, if what they told you is true, someone else dies and they declare general mourning for the whole planet. I don't get it."

Nico shrugged and kept looking at Charlie. They stared at each other in silence for a few minutes, sharing the same unspoken feelings of incomprehension, helplessness, and impotence that were almost customary now. Charlie ended the moment by slapping her thighs twice.

"I'm out of here, see if I can find out what's going on."

"Charlie!"

"What?"

"Are you leaving me here by myself?"

"It's only a funeral, Nico. You said so yourself. Don't tell me you're afraid of ghosts, are you? You've always been so macho."

"Lady, go fuck yourself!"

Ankhjaia'langtxhrl, Ankkhaia to humans, was striding toward Lake Htor where he was to meet Hithrolgh, the first among the three beings he cared about most in the world. They had shared their entire childhood and part of their youth until their lives had to take separate paths after their final classification. For one whole Xhroll year, during the time young adults are considered to be sexually mature, they had attempted the difficult task of reproduction over and over again, by themselves and with other couples. When the year was over, Ankhjaia'langtxhrl, having managed to implant in one partner, had become an ari-arkhj. Hithrolgh, who managed neither to implant nor be implanted, had been officially classified as a xhrea for life. Nevertheless, their relationship had continued the same as always.

They hadn't been able to see each other for a few trips now, and Ankhjaia'langtxhrl was anxiously waiting to meet Hithrolgh and hear the news he was so hungry for.

Over the years, while Ankhjaia'langtxhrl focused on fulfilling an ari-arkhj's duty to provide Xhroll with a hol'la, traveling aboard cargo ships looking for the chance to establish contact with xhri who could become abbas, Hithrolgh had been rising in the hierarchy to become the fifth member of the Xhri Affairs Council.

A social change was happening on Xhroll, so serious a change that not even the abbas could ignore it. And with every return to Xhroll, Ankhjaia'langtxhrl's anxiety increased. The social structure that had been set in stone since childhood was in danger of crumbling every time the xhreas made a move, for they had all the power, despite the preferential treatment accorded to the abbas and the ari-arkhjs.

Xhroll's long day had just begun when Ankhjaia'langtxhrl climbed up the hill overlooking the lake. A large opalescent, rose-tinted area spread out below, the grass looking grayish in the early morning light.

Standing still on top of a rock, staring vacantly into the distant southern mountains, Hithrolgh awaited, shorn of the short black wig used in public and dressed in an iridescent tunic that etched a graceful figure against the mist. Hithrolgh had very light green eyes, copper-colored skin, and, as typical for the Xhroll, a face and body that had undergone several surgical procedures to adjust to the classic standard: small straight nose, wide shoulders, narrow hips. Turning around when Ankhaia'langtxhrl approached, Hithrolgh said:

"I'm so happy to see you, Ankhjaia'langtxhrl. I've really missed you this time."

Ankhjaia'langtxhrl moved closer and they stood face to face staring into each other's eyes for a few seconds.

"I haven't missed you this time, Hithrolgh. It has been an interesting and productive trip."

"Xhroll is grateful to you. I am, too. In these times, a life is worth double. If the hol'la is viable, we're safe."

"If we can count on the xhris' cooperation, that is?"

Hithrolgh remained silent for a moment.

"I want you to know this. The council thinks that the xhris' cooperation, their voluntary consent, is not absolutely essential. According to your reports, they do not react positively to life."

"The xhri ari-arkhj says they are able to have offspring whenever they want, that they are overpopulated, and therefore they willingly render themselves useless, either permanently or temporarily."

"We cannot allow a potential and necessary life to be wasted. We must assure our survival. We need to increase our population."

Ankhjaia'langtxhrl looked at Hithrolgh, noting a growing feeling of surprise. Hithrolgh's tone of voice had a different quality, similar to how humans sounded when stating something that was different from what they were thinking.

"Hithrolgh, when you say 'we' who are you referring to?"

"To Xhroll."

"The whole of Xhroll or only the xhreas?"

"I mean Xhroll as a whole, but you must understand we xhreas are the most threatened. We cannot reproduce."

"But in return you have full decision-making power."

"That's not true." Hithrolgh stood up and started to walk, knowing Ankhjaia'langtxhrl would follow. "Traditionally, the highest member of every major council is an ari-arkhj."

"There aren't that many ari-arkhjs."

"There aren't that many major councils either."

A tense silence set in. Hithrolgh kept looking doggedly at the mountains while Ankhjaia'langtxhrl tried hard to meet the other's eyes, without success.

"In the past it was a pleasure interacting with you, Hithrolgh."

"In the past we did not have so many responsibilities, and our duties were not so different. In the past you, too, were a xhrea."

"Do you want me to feel guilty for being an ari-arkhj?"

"That would be absurd."

"Sometimes I think normal xhrea behavior is becoming absurd."

"That hurts me, Ankhjaia'langtxhrl."

"It hurts me too, what you are doing to us. Everything was different before. Everyone had their own place in life. Now, you xhreas have taken over completely. From the day I got my pectoral muscles implanted, every time I return from a trip I get the feeling that there's no longer any place in society for us or our abbas. You treat us like goods to be managed, not like full-fledged beings with rights."

"I believe you've been interacting too much with the xhris. Your thoughts are getting polluted."

"And who is polluting yours?"

"It's exasperating. It's like building a house on sand. We are completely dependent on the abbas and on you. You have to understand our point of view. We cannot allow an abba to refuse to reproduce. Or an ari-arkhj to bond with an abba exclusively and for life. That is a social crime."

"Has that actually occurred?"

"Yes."

"That's profoundly disturbing. But those transgressions must be rare. A few pathological cases."

"It is an organized, underground resistance movement, Ankhjaia'langtxhrl. We know that for certain, and I was hoping you could provide me with information about it."

Ankhjaia'langtxhrl was unable to respond, recalling with a shudder the rumors about the internment of abbas in secret locations. "Is it true that you are restricting the freedoms of certain groups of abbas and ari-arkhjs?"

"I don't deal with internal affairs, you know that. I am in charge of looking for xhri abbas. I sent you on that mission and we got lucky. I don't know about anything else."

"Answer my question. Is it true you all are planning to turn us into breeding animals?"

"We hope to find a solution to this issue by using xhri abbas like yours. If the hol'la turns out to be viable, you won't have to worry anymore."

"And if it doesn't?"

"You alone can guarantee our survival."

"And what about you? What is your role?"

"We xhreas have created Xhroll, Ankhjaia'langtxhrl. Whole generations of us reclaimed the planet from the ruins left behind by the Firsts and rebuilt it into the habitable world we now have. You and the abbas give life to the xhreas, but it is we who make the world turn. We who are not burdened by bonds of affection or sexual compulsions, who only compete to become ever better at our jobs, who love Xhroll above all else. We xhreas: thinking beings whose brains are not subject to hormonal changes, who don't commit violence against ourselves, who have had the fortune to become the next phase in evolution."

"An evolution toward infertility and death."

"Not if we are united."

"Yes, Hithrolgh. Even united. We get fewer abbas with every new generation. In one or two more, our whole population will be xhreas, with a few ari-arkhjs here and there, and then what are you planning to do with that superior brain of yours?"

"If the earthlings turn out to be viable, the extinction of our abbas won't be an issue. It may even solve many conflicts."

"And what happens if they don't want us to implant?"

"Did your xhri abba want to?

"No. But now they are aware of what may happen."

"There are almost three hundred abbas on the Terran base. Not counting their ari-arkhjs, in about twenty xhri years there will be five thousand new lives. Maybe they won't like it at first, but they will get used to it. To give life is beautiful."

"And what about Earth World's reaction?"

"They are overpopulated. We are very far away. They believe we have powerful weapons. Nothing will happen."

"They do have weapons, Hithrolgh. They will come to Xhroll and demolish it."

"I don't think so. But, anyway, Xhroll was destroyed once before and we survived it. Our reproductive structure was altered, but we survived."

Ankhjaia'langtxhrl stepped closer and gently placed a hand on Hithrolgh's shoulder, knowing full well what that meant.

"Aren't you afraid, Hithrolgh? Doesn't the world we are creating frighten you?"

"Do not touch me, Ankhjaia'langtxhrl. I am not an abba."

"We've known each other forever. Let me get close to you. Let everything be as it was before, even just for a moment."

"I cannot. I do not want to."

"I need it, Hithrolgh."

"You have your abba. You have the hol'la. You have the xhri's ari-arkhj. You have more than I have ever had. Don't ask me for anything."

"You said you had missed me."

"I was wrong. What I missed was my memory of Ankhjaia'langtxhrl. You are not that. You've changed. I have, too. Your current way of thinking is incompatible with my own. You're a danger to us."

"You mean you're going to exile me from Xhroll or throw me in an internment camp to produce more xhreas?"

"I will not be part of whatever decision is reached."

"I prefer exile, Hithrolgh."

"I will keep that in mind, if the occasion arises."

"What will happen to the humans? Will they return to their world?"

"I don't know."

"They matter to me."

"Xhroll comes first. You know that."

"Xhroll comes first."

Their eyes met for an instant before they quickly averted them.

"I would have liked not to be a xhrea, Ankhjaia'langtxhrl, but that's what I am."

"I understand, Hithrolgh. But I am not."

They parted ways knowing they would probably never see each other again. Not under friendly circumstances, anyway. All of a sudden Ankhjaia'langtxhrl had become a nuisance, one of those rare individuals disrupting the smooth running of Xhroll's social machine. Ankkhaia had turned from model citizen into troublemaker just by expressing doubts and opinions to a person known since childhood, part of his three-member core group. And that was a terrible development. If one couldn't express an opinion without fear anymore, something was very wrong.

It hurt to think of how Hithrolgh had changed, becoming inflexible and bigoted regarding sexual beings. It was clearly due to fear. All xhreas were afraid of them and that was why they tried to control them, to keep them under their power. And the worst part was that history showed fear led to cruelty, which was justified in the name of the common good. The xhreas' common good.

The humans knew nothing about all that. They were convinced that when the hol'la was born they would go back to their world, to that wonderful world where everything was so easy, where only two kinds of beings existed and both had a reproductive function. They were equal in duties and privileges just as, according to the experts, it had been on Xhroll before the start of the New Era and the changes it had brought.

Ankkhaia didn't want to lose that close friendship with Hithrolgh but had no wish to harm the humans either. Equally unacceptable was the thought of finishing life on a breeding farm to satisfy the xhreas' expansionist desires.

Reaching the elevator door closest to Charlie's quarters, Ankkhaia took a long blond wig out of a closet and put it on without checking the monitor, knowing the green eyes it reflected would be a reminder of those other green eyes so recently lost. Then, once inside the elevator, Ankkhaia made the decision he'd been wrestling with before meeting Hithrolgh. He had thought of consulting Hithrolgh, but the turn the conversation had taken convinced him otherwise. Hithrolgh would disagree, that was clear, so the only solution was to act without having asked anyone's opinion. If the xhreas could change certain norms for the sake of certain interests, an ari-arkhj could, too.

Ankkhaia took me to see the dead.

It may be a bit over the top to say it like that. She took me to see one of them, a member of her core group, which is the closest thing they have to our concept of family here. A xhrea who died four years ago while on a space mission.

On Xhroll the dead are placed in a kind of armored crypt at the very center of the planet. It takes hours to descend all the way down there and you have to do tons of health-related paperwork before you're granted the electronic license required to access the final stretch of the road down.

From the last elevator stop, visitors must still cover several miles through a labyrinth of crisscrossed cells, like tiny metal rooms, filled with thousands of cadavers that, in appearance at least, are as beyond hope as any dead body back home. And yet they're endowed with a type of life that lets them continue to be useful to Xhroll as long as their minds are still connected to those of living beings.

From what I've been told, not all dead bodies are preserved. If those who died had no expertise usable after life ended, their corpses are buried in a place of their choice. If, on the other hand, they met their deaths while conducting an important experiment, or if they held special, valuable knowledge, there's an attempt to retain their minds and their spirits? souls? so they can continue to contribute to Xhroll's survival.

Sometimes, there's simply nothing that can be done to maintain contact and there's no choice but to resign oneself and accept a death as final. That's when the planet observes a day of mourning.

I've got the impression that this practice pricks at their consciences, that they know—or feel, or think—that it isn't fair for those who should have died to be sequestered in that excuse of a life. But they must do so, because of the population shortage.

I don't know why (it's a taboo subject and I can't just bring it up point blank), but it seems they don't focus their research on reproductive or fertility issues, but instead direct all their efforts on the science of death.

Leaving the elevator behind, Ankkhaia and I walked in silence for twenty minutes, turning right and left through perfectly lit hallways where our bodies didn't cast any shadow. Our footsteps sounded faint, muffled by the textile floor and wall coverings, and I could feel my pulse beating in my temples. I can't say I was scared, but I did feel a vague sense of danger, of tension, as if I'd suddenly become aware I was on an alien planet millions of miles away from my own, walking alone next to an extraterrestrial through a maze of twisting corridors, tons of rock over my head and thousands of not-quite-dead dead bodies all around me.

When we got to the cell we were looking for my hands were trembling, my whole body was damp and cold, and my mouth was so dry I couldn't even clear my throat.

I'm not sure what I was expecting.

I'm not sure if I was surprised.

The xhrea was standing upright in a lighted niche, like a coffin made of glass, like an old-fashioned telephone booth. There was no maintenance equipment of any kind. No wires, needles, or any other item a human would associate with clinics and hospitals.

Her eyes were open, light green, just like Ankkhaia's. The deadest eyes I've ever seen.

She was naked and, although her chest was flat, the absence of pubic hair made it clear she was a woman, like Ankkhaia, like me. They had shaved her head. Her skin had a slight bluish tint, like a piece of porcelain at a museum, without a single hair, without a single shadow. My mind recalled the Xhroll who'd been smashed to bits against the rocks, and for a moment I had to make an effort not to howl when I imagined his living dead body in the glass booth.

"Now you've seen him," said Ankkhaia, turning toward me.

"Can you speak with her?"

"With him. Yes, of course."

I couldn't believe someone could speak with that piece of morgue-flesh.

"And what do you talk about?"

She stared at me, as she always did, without me understanding if it had any meaning at all.

"I speak to him. He speaks, through the net, about issues that matter to Xhroll. I come to bring him a bit of life. I and everyone else. We come to offer the only thing the dead are able to appreciate: memories, visions, words."

I believe I shook my head, dizzy. Ankkhaia, following my teachings on body language, interpreted it as a denial.

"It is so, Charlie. It's the truth. Leave us alone now."

I stepped out of the cell, leaned against the wall, and let myself slowly slide down to the floor and into a crouching position, arms wrapped around my legs, head resting on top.

I thought it was gruesome. Simply gruesome. Perverse. Twisted. I just couldn't help it.

Inside, Ankkhaia was using a voice I'd never heard before, full of inflections and nuances. It could have been the same language I'd been learning, but it wasn't. It was the other one, the one coming from the loudspeakers, infinitely older and richer, as Ankkhaia had already explained to me. It was in that ritual language that she was talking to that blue, open-eyed cadaver.

She used that absurd lingo they use in everyday life, the one they'd taught us, for what she told me later. She spoke of the sparkle of light on the snow-covered mountain sides of the first home they'd shared; of a new kind of blue-flowered wild primrose they'd succeeded in acclimating to the shores of Lake Htor; of the white coral reef that had grown big enough to shelter a lagoon as smooth and rosy as a polar dawn.

She spoke in words unknown to me, soft and sweet, full of vowels. They brought to mind the echoes of a shared past, a life connected to nature, dedicated to loving thousands of beings, as if by joining all their souls together they imbued Xhroll with a soul.

She spoke with a sweetness and a passion I would never have thought possible; a passion that gave me chills. To me, a human. And the whole time she called him "ahalaiaia," a word I thought was obsolete and means something like "brother of the heart."

I risked taking a look inside. Ankkhaia was hugging the cadaver, whose lifeless eyes were watching me over her shoulder. I returned to my place in the hallway, not wanting to see anything else, as I heard her say in the common tongue:

"Keep on suffering for Xhroll, brother. We need it. We need you. If the future turns out to be as we plan, you will soon be free. Have faith, brother. Be brave. For Xhroll."

I heard the soft click of the lid closing and Ankkhaia's labored breathing gradually easing. When everything went quiet, she stepped back into the hallway where I was waiting far enough away for her not to get the impression that I'd been spying on her.

"We can leave."

I must have made some kind of noise with my throat, because she added:

"Do you want to ask something?"

I was just about to shake my head no when it struck me that there sure was something I wanted to know, something that might alleviate, even a little, that horror.

"What kind of job did your . . .? I mean . . . What kind of information could be so valuable as to do that to someone?"

I had the vague impression she was glad I understood the suffering a dead being had to endure to keep connected to life, but I may have imagined it. The Xhroll are so inexpressive, you find yourself constantly projecting your own emotions onto them.

"He made contact with two other species within our galaxy before having an accident. He was the only crewmember Xhroll was able to recover. One of those two species is yours. He and the spaceship he was travelling in established first contact. The other species is unknown to us, and the information is vital because he alone is in possession of it. And it must be very important if they made the decision to downgrade contact with Earth World in favor of pursuing the other one."

I was stunned.

"Are there other intelligent humanoid species in the galaxy?"

"There are five, as far as we know, besides Xhroll and humans. Are you surprised?"

I nodded my head slowly.

"It's strange. Nico knew that and she didn't seem surprised."

"Nico knew that?"

For the thousandth time I felt the urgent desire to strangle that bastard. But it only lasted a second. I quickly realized he'd probably forgotten it or, maybe for reasons related to his own pride, he'd chosen to forget. It's better that way. The truth is, I'm not at all interested in Nico knowing certain things. For instance, Nico doesn't need to know that on Xhroll the dead are not quite dead.

MALES AND FEMALES

Nights were very long for Nico Andrade. Despite the baths, massages, relaxing aromas, and nutritious food, the hours would slip by and either he would get no sleep at all, or he would fall into such a deep slumber that, upon waking, he'd feel as if he'd been dead. And when he was able to sleep, his dreams were filled with nightmares, inhabited by warm, slippery monsters the color of blood that slid down between his legs, searching for a place to enter him and seize him by the bowels.

He would often wake up in complete darkness with his hands clamped over his mouth stifling a scream, slick with sweat and smelling of fear. After that, he would sprawl out on the bed, face up, eyes open, trying to imagine the body he used to have: lithe, strong, unique. Macho.

Now, he didn't really know what he was. The Xhroll had turned him into a shapeless mass of flesh stuffed full of hormones that cried for no reason and wrung its hands, that overflowed with desire at the thought of a flan topped with whipped cream, that couldn't think for fifteen minutes straight about anything requiring mental effort. The Xhroll. No word could possibly be more offensive than that. The word *Xhroll* was already ominous enough, because it was everything. Everything.

He realized his hands were falling asleep, and as he sat up to massage his arms tears pooled unexpectedly behind his lashes and flowed down his unshaven cheeks. He felt alone, abandoned, vulnerable. If only there was someone there next to him! But he had never liked that. It was all well and good to have company in bed while you were awake, but once you'd finished your "prime directive," it was best if the girl had the good sense to head back to her own bed and let you sleep in peace. He'd never understood how a person could sleep while hugging an unfamiliar body, subjected to the gaze of someone who moments before had been your hookup—your lover in "proper" speech—and who now would revert back to what she was: a complete stranger judging you while you were defenseless. His way was better for both parties, it was what was right. There was no good reason to put up with someone else's snoring, their smells, their habits, their red eyes and jaundiced skin sitting across from you at the breakfast table.

As he rubbed his arms, Nico thought about his mother. For the first time in twenty years, he remembered her intensely, with nostalgia, needing her. The only woman who could help him now, who could console him. The only woman for whom he didn't have to be Lieutenant Nicodemo Andrade, lone wolf and perfect stud.

The thought embarrassed him and he pushed it aside. He didn't need anyone, never did. He was going to get through all of this, alone, and then he'd leave the Fleet for good. He'd buy himself a yacht with his pension and spend his time hauling rich tourists around the Caribbean to fish for tuna. If there were any. Tuna, that is. There'd always be rich tourists. And brunettes with long flowing hair and velvety eyes. And smiling redheads, sprinkled with freckles. Cute girls with chestnut hair, masculine hips, and big round tits. And petite Asian girls, with almost blue hair and mysterious looks, deliciously narrow-hipped.

But what he would never, ever in his life consider doing again—and this was a solemn oath—was screw a green-eyed blonde. Never ever. For as long as he lived. Never.

Charlie Fonseca passed through the rooms and corridors that led to Nico's quarters with the ease of someone who'd done it many times before, smiling at the service personnel and the abbas that crossed her path. She knew from Ankkhaia that smiling was a gesture unfamiliar to the Xhroll, but so far she'd not been able to control the natural impulse to smile and nod when passing someone. Fortunately, the Xhroll didn't take it as an insult, just a strange tic lacking any significance, the same way a human might interpret someone sticking a finger in their ear or placing their hand behind their head. She had asked Ankkhaia what the Xhroll equivalent to smiling would be, and she answered, as seriously as always, that when a Xhroll felt happy they expressed it with words. "We are a society that mastered verbal expression thousands of years ago," she had responded. "We have no need to supplement our words with other signs. Our language is sufficiently precise." Charlie had laughed, again confusing Ankkhaia.

Ankkhaia was funny, in her way; funny without knowing it and without meaning to be. Charlie was liking her better all the time. Since their visit with the dead, Charlie had felt that they'd crossed an invisible threshold, that Ankkhaia was becoming her friend—just about. They had exchanged some details about their personal lives. Pretending that it was a chance encounter,

Ankkhaia had showed her a group of children working outside with a botany professor and had insinuated that life on Xhroll was not as idyllic as one might think, something to do with the xhreas and their concept of society.

Charlie, in return, had shared some information about how human society functioned, the assignment of social roles, the languages of Earth, human attitudes regarding life and death, all things that Ankkhaia wanted to know more about.

She liked Ankkhaia. She was so clear, so direct, and so amusing in her way, that for the first time in years, Charlie felt that she'd found a friend. They enjoyed their time together. They taught each other a lot, and even though they hadn't talked about anything personal yet, Charlie thought that would happen in time. For now, there were too many broad topics to cover and, unfortunately, too many that couldn't be discussed. As was customary in diplomatic assignments, her orders were fairly ambiguous, yet crystal clear about one thing: she was to learn as much as possible about the Xhroll while revealing a minimal amount of information in return. She constantly had to monitor those trifling comments so as not to accidentally reveal anything that could be damaging to the idea the Xhroll were forming about Earth.

Much easier said than done, of course. How was she going to ask Ankkhaia about the type of weapons the Xhroll had without being prepared to reciprocate? She always kept her eyes and ears open, but even on Earth nobody simply bumps into nuclear missiles on street corners.

In any case, she was in an excellent mood. It seemed like things were finally moving forward, and every moment brought them closer to the big event that would send them back home.

She had no wish to visit the lieutenant, but it was the only way to make sure everything was going smoothly. If all was as expected, it wouldn't take more than ten minutes.

Charlie entered Nico's room with a deep breath and the most radiant smile she could muster. Nico, settled in a floating chair next to the television, which was their name for a Xhroll device that used a system similar to VR on Earth to display virtual scenery, was staring blankly at a black sand desert on the shores of a pale blue sea in which some animals were leaping and diving too quickly to be recognized.

"I have to get out of here, Charlie," he said without turning to look at her. "I'm going crazy."

Charlie approached him slowly, her mind racing. She placed her hands on his shoulders, and despite clearly feeling his rejection through the sheer fabric of his white jumpsuit, maintained the pressure and began to massage his muscles, which felt like hardened rubber.

"I'll talk with Ankkhaia to see if they'll let you take a walk outside."

He shook his head.

"I want to go home, Charlie." He turned to face her and only then did she realize how sunken his eyes were, the paleness of his skin.

She stroked his unshaven cheek, trying not to call attention to the tears glistening in his eyes.

"I'm going crazy, Charlie. I've started talking to myself, you know?"

"Come on! That's normal, we all talk to ourselves sometimes."

Nico turned back to the television.

"It's moving now."

Charlie watched the screen closely, but the only thing moving there were the aquatic animals. Because Nico wasn't connected to the machine, he couldn't be feeling anything from it that she wasn't.

"What's moving, Nico?" she asked softly.

He started to cry, large tears that went sliding down his cheeks and fell onto his chest.

"It's been happening for three weeks. I hadn't told you yet."

"But that's fantastic! Doesn't it feel amazing? Let's see, let me feel."

She knelt down next to him and placed her hand on his belly, waiting.

"It must be sleeping. I don't feel anything."

He covered his mouth with his hand, trying to stifle the escaping sobs that were making his whole body shake.

"Nico! Nico, what's wrong? This is fabulous! It means that everything is going well, and that it'll only be a little longer, you're more than halfway there. And anyway, isn't it fun to feel it move? Don't you wait a while after you feel the first kick, hoping it'll move again? Don't you feel like laughing and talking with him or her?"

"What do you know about it? You've never been through this. It isn't fabulous. It's . . . it's disgusting. It's like having a live animal trapped inside you looking for the most vulnerable place to gnaw its way out. It's the worst feeling in the world. You can't imagine it. I wish a real woman would've been sent with me, who would've understood me, who would've known what it was like!"

Charlie got up and stood contemplating the black sand desert. The silence was becoming thick and heavy.

"I know what I'm talking about, Nico," she said, finally.

"You? You, too . . .?"

"It was so long ago . . . I was only eighteen years old. I had just started at the Academy. With a scholarship. My family was really conservative. Fundamentalists. And at that age I was still fertile. I lied on my forms; it didn't occur to any doctors that a woman of my age might not have been sterilized. I thought that if I kept away from men there wouldn't be a problem. And there wasn't. I soon got a reputation as being cold and stuck-up."

There was a long pause, as if Charlie were fighting against the words she was saying.

"They raped me. I got pregnant. I lost the scholarship. I spent a year living off maternity benefits. Alone. Humiliated. Hating myself and hating the thing I carried inside of me. I refused psychological therapy, I refused everything. I almost didn't eat. My whole future had tanked, understand? Same for my entire way of looking at the world, my ideals, the ideals I had developed in opposition to my family. Turns out they were right, the world is terrible, people are bad, and men are monsters. God is all-powerful and punishes. That kind of thing."

She ran her hand across her forehead as if to tear out the thoughts that had been forming there.

"And the baby boy or girl?" asked Nico in a thin voice.

"It was a boy. He died at birth. He died at birth."

Nico said nothing. He buried his head in his hands, unable to look at her.

"I was happy, though. That was the worst part. I was happy." Charlie continued struggling to form the words, which came out dry, bitter, as if she were spitting them out. "I thought I had gotten lucky, that I could go back and do something worthwhile with my life. And there you have it . . . Ever since then I've been asking myself what it would have been like if he had lived, if I had a twenty-three year old son right now, an adult person who would be closer to me than any other person has ever been.

"He was the cutest baby. And he was mine, Nico. Mine."

"Did they let you back into the Space Academy?" asked Nico when the silence got too painful.

"Into the Space Intelligence Service. They know how to use the hate and frustration of a twenty-year-old woman there."

"Are you a spy?" Nico's voice sounded more offended than surprised.

"Something like that. In real life it's less romantic."

"What do you do aboard the *Victoria*?"

Charlie shrugged lightly.

"The same thing I do here. The same thing I've always done. Watch, listen, inform."

"About us?"

She gave no answer.

"That's why they sent you here with me, huh? Not to give me moral support or anything like that. To spy. On me and on them, right?"

"Let's drop this, Nico. Please."

He got up with some difficulty and approached her slowly, a pathetic figure with his swollen belly and the black line of his mustache crossing his face.

They regarded each other for a few seconds.

"They used both of us," said Nico at last.

"We all use one another. It doesn't matter."

They embraced softly, each looking for a little warmth and companionship in the body of the other. Gradually they began to snuggle, and then shyly kiss.

"I'm so alone, Charlie!" he murmured in her ear. "And I'm so scared."

She sighed and hugged him tighter.

"We're all alone."

"Stay with me, please. Please."

Charlie took him by the waist and guided him toward the bed. She had no idea how to treat the fragile, wounded creature Andrade had become. She felt trapped in that alien room, with this human she'd shared so much with, precisely because he was human. She wanted to get out of there, to deny with a wave of her hand the existence of Andrade and of the new being that only the Xhroll wanted, to head for the surface of this unspoiled planet and forget about everything.

She laid Andrade down on the bed, trying to close herself off from his hangdog expression, feeling like a parent putting a child to bed, ignoring their fear of the dark, telling them that monsters don't exist. An adult that leaves their child behind a closed door, knowing what's hiding in the closet but unable to face it.

"Everything will be fine, Nico. You rest." She passed a hand over his forehead, parting the locks of dark hair that had grown in the weeks since they'd been far from the Fleet and its regulations.

She turned to leave but found that he had attached himself to the pocket of her jumpsuit in an attempt to keep her next to him. She looked at him, exasperated with his insistence and his childishness, and couldn't look away from those pleading eyes.

She had never been able to understand men. In spite of the official opinion that mandated the complete absence of sex-based discrimination, every time she had treated a man the same way she would a woman it had been a mistake.

"What do you want from me, Nico?" she muttered, almost inaudibly. "Don't you see I have nothing to give you?"

He kept quiet without taking his eyes off hers.

"Do you want to fuck? Is that it?"

He lowered his gaze and twisted a piece of fabric between his fingers, shaking his head no.

"No, Charlie. For once, that's not it." His attempt to smile seemed bitter. "I can't. I haven't been able to for weeks, but I wouldn't want to even if I could. You all think that for men it's the solution to every problem." He paused for a moment, searching for the words to express what he was feeling. "What I wanted was . . . forget it. You don't have it."

"What is it?"

"Forget it. It's stupid."

"What is it?"

"Love."

He raised his eyes and for a moment they looked at each other like strangers, like they didn't belong to the same species. Then, slowly, they began laughing without breaking eye contact. Charlie took off her jumpsuit, letting it fall at her feet, and got into bed with Nico.

"I told you, I can't."

"We'll see."

From the bed, Charlie heard Nico's voice as he sang in the shower, a Xhroll invention, a special courtesy for humans that sprayed water from all sides at once and paused at random intervals for varying durations. He had to yell pretty loudly for her to hear what he was saying, but it seemed like he had recovered his booming voice and self-confidence. Charlie answered in mono-syllables, amazed that what had started as a simple act of charity had become such a gratifying experience.

When Nico returned to the room, naked and smiling, Charlie noticed for the first time how big his belly had gotten in the last few days.

"You're a miracle, Charlie. I'll never be able to thank you enough for this, girl. You've given me back my dignity."

He sat down on the bed beside her and kissed her hair. Charlie smiled.

"I swear, I've never understood why men, after so many centuries of art, philosophy, and other trivialities, still believe their dignity lies at the tip of their dick."

Nico burst into laughter.

"Well maybe not for artists and philosophers, but seeing as I'm just a simple mechanic . . ."

Charlie found herself smiling at Nico with a fondness she hadn't believed she was capable of when it came to him, and it worried her. She jumped out of bed and started getting dressed hurriedly. She wasn't willing to allow herself feelings of school-girl sentimentality or inopportune crushes. Andrade was her responsibility and she would take care of him as much as possible without risking anything, without giving any part of herself. In her experience, there was nothing worse than falling for somebody who, deep down, you despise as a person.

"Where are you off to?" Nico had just realized Charlie was almost out the door.

"I'm going for a walk. I'm meeting with Ankkhaia later, we still have lots to teach each other."

"Charlie, have you noticed that in spite of the fact almost all of the staff here are men, it seems like the women are the ones giving orders?"

Charlie bit her lower lip and thought about it for a minute.

"I don't know. It seems like we're making a mistake in our judgment somewhere. I just don't see them as men or as women."

"Oh really? Well, how do you see them then?"

She considered it again for a moment and shrugged.

"Weird," she said at last.

Nico started laughing.

"Yes. Weird is exactly what they are."

"I'll see you later, Nico."

"Bye!"

Charlie left, thinking that there were lots of things she didn't understand. Too many. And more all the time.

Nico lay on the bed with a dreamy expression on his face, his left hand resting on his belly, his right cupping his genitals.

In that moment he felt comfortable in his own skin. In spite of the alien environment, of the thing he was carrying inside of himself that he couldn't ignore, of the uncertainty regarding his future, at that moment Nico felt at peace with himself. He owed that to Charlie. Or if not to her directly, at least to the fact that for once she'd behaved like a real woman with him, not like the remote, somewhat caustic captain he'd gotten to know in the last few weeks.

It always seemed strange to him, that change that happened in women as soon as you'd gotten them in bed, as if they'd suddenly realized that all of the centuries of fighting for gender equality were nothing more than an intellectual ploy by the dissatisfied to rob the human female of her true purpose, her natural role of submission to men, to their protection and their desire.

He stretched out luxuriously on the bed, half-lamenting Charlie's absence. If she had still been there, he would have liked to go another round, even if it was only to prove to himself that his problems, at least his temporary impotence, had really gone away. Charlie was good in bed. Aggressive, but sweet. Attentive to shared pleasure, not like those stupid girls who fake orgasms thinking the guy wouldn't notice and believing that deep down he didn't care. Not Charlie. Charlie was exacting of her own pleasure, and it was satisfying to give it to her to increase his own. He'd gotten lucky with her. A woman with experience and common sense. From now on, life would be much more bearable.

Charlie, like every other woman he'd been with in his life, and he'd certainly lost count, had in her a secret lock that could only be opened with a magic key. Sometimes it even surprised him that it always worked, that it worked with them all. And he had that key. It was a simple word that at times should be accompanied by an act, and at others worked on its own. The word was "love," a miraculous "open, sesame" that unlocked the gates to the cave of treasures. He only had to say it with conviction, believing in its power, and every obstacle was knocked down. Even with Charlie.

Something moved inside of him and Nico had to make an effort not to scream. The damn creature had woken up and now it was starting its workout so it would be in shape when it came time to emerge. The Xhroll had explained to him that as soon as the creature's developmental profile indicated that it was mature enough, they would perform surgery under total anesthesia to extract it, but they couldn't predict with certainty when that moment would come, as the Xhroll had a gestation period of some seven months, while humans needed ten lunar cycles, almost eight weeks more.

He got out of bed and started to browse the landscapes on the television, looking for something that would distract him enough to forget the terror he felt each time he considered the possibility that the beast would decide to come out before it was time, before the tests indicated that it was ready for surgery. He hadn't been able to forget how he'd felt that night, the pain that tore his belly like a serrated knife, the blood spilling between his legs in hot, sticky surges, his whole body throbbing. What would happen if the Xhroll did nothing and just left the creature to hack a path for itself until it reached the outside world at the cost of the life of its host? After all, they had no interest in his life. Then they could communicate to Earth that there'd been complications with the birth, and that unfortunately Lieutenant Andrade had not survived. Who was going to stop them?

Charlie, maybe. Or Ankkhaia, who was a real bitch, but who seemed to take her duties as protector pretty seriously, visiting him even against his will and bringing him small gifts that he had never accepted.

He felt a chill, but didn't bother asking anyone to turn up the heat. He knew from experience that the ideal temperature for an abba was 20 degrees Celsius and nothing he could do or say would change that by a single degree. He had already tried it, and it had ended with him punching his bed out of sheer impotence, which had earned him a mild sedative that kept him staring at the ceiling with a silly grin on his face for three whole days. Anger in an abba's body wasn't good for the development of the hol'la. If humans thought the same thing, there probably wouldn't be a single living baby left on the planet.

He shot a look at the Xhroll clock, which he had finally learned to read, and started to get dressed. Soon they would come to take him to an interrogation session, psychotherapy, as they called it, during which a Xhroll (always a different one, though they could have been the same, just with different hair and different-colored eyes) would question him thoroughly about the previous few hours of his life. Once, he had asked why the psychiatrist, or whatever it was, was always different, and the answer, seemingly off the cuff, had been that it was Xhroll that asked the questions and cared about the health and development of its abbas and hol'las, and not a specific individual. Nico had tried to explain that to humans it's important to establish a personal relationship with the specialists who follow your progress, and they had told him that was what he had an ari-arkhj for, two of them in his particular case. Then there was nothing more to do. The questions began.

Just then the door opened, and two Xhroll entered to fetch him with the same lack of expression common to all Xhroll and without a single word of greeting. Nico shrugged, positioned himself between the two of them as usual, and allowed them to lead him to his floating chair. But this time the path they took was different than usual; his escorts turned to the right every time they reached a junction in the hallways, which started to take them farther and farther from the familiar routes.

"Where are you taking me?" Nico finally asked, growing increasingly uneasy.

The Xhroll, as usual, didn't move a single muscle or give any impression that they'd heard his question.

"Where are we going, dammit?"

Nothing. Complete silence, save for the soft shuffle of their black felt shoes.

They entered a room that could have been the same one they'd just left, but Nico knew it wasn't. They helped him down from the chair with all necessary deference and withdrew

without a word. The door solidified behind them, and somehow Nico realized, with absolute certainty, that they had just
taken him prisoner.

Hithrolgh entered the room quietly and headed to the place
waiting for him in the circle. Only another Xhroll would have
sensed in his leisurely, assured movements the urgency of the
situation.

"Report, Hithrolgh," requested one of the Xhroll present.

Hithrolgh swept his gaze over the gathered faces. All of
them were xhreas, all five.

"One member is absent."

"That member could not be contacted in time."

"So this meeting does not conform to regulation."

"The situation demands it. The turn of events is
unprecedented."

Hithrolgh hesitated for a moment, his appearance betraying none of the emotions he was feeling, and began giving a
brief summary of the conversation that he had just had with
Ankhjaia'langtxhrl, without mentioning the personal aspects
of the exchange.

"This means that the ari-arkhjs have begun to suspect the
xhreas and are mounting a resistance, though shallow, to the
plans for the future of Xhroll."

"I must add, though it pains me, that my impression is that
Ankhjaia'langtxhrl does not speak for the ari-arkhjs but only
for himself."

"This is not possible."

"Yes it is. We all know that for some time the ari-arkhjs, and
evidently their abbas, have been evolving dangerously toward a

more primitive individualism, to the detriment of the species."

"In the case of Ankhjaia'langtxhrl, it's very possible this is because of his relationship with the xhris."

"And how do you explain the other deviants on the planet?"

"They fear us. They believe that we are the deviants."

"Nonsense! We are Xhroll."

"As are they." Hithrolgh's words, which had sprung from his mouth almost of their own accord, created a tense silence in the room.

"That is evident. But sexed creatures are incapable of thinking with clarity, especially in times of crisis. Their hormonal processes impede their reasoning. Only we are in the position to think with clarity and make the best decisions for Xhroll."

Another hush fell over the room.

"Three of us are still unaware of the new situation we are facing. I request your complete attention. Something unprecedented has just occurred in the relations between the xhri abba and its ari-arkhj."

"Ankhjaia'langtxhrl?" The concern in Hithrolgh's voice did not go unnoticed by any of those present.

"The one called Charlie."

"That is comforting."

"I do not believe your feelings will be the same when you hear this information. The xhris have just finished copulating for purely sexual reasons."

"The ari-arkhj tried to implant an abba that was already implanted?"

"I don't believe my statement left any room for doubt."

"To what end?"

"We don't know."

This time the silence held a quality of horror and confusion. Every xhrea felt momentarily paralyzed by the monstrosity of the situation.

"The xhri abba has been confined someplace else until we come to a decision. Its two ari-arkhj have not yet been informed."

Four of those present, Hithrolgh among them, removed a tube of sedative lotion from a pocket of their jumpsuits and rubbed a dab carefully into each wrist before continuing the discussion.

"An abba and an ari-arkhj may not be separated without the express consent of the latter."

"We all know the rules, but these rules were made when a situation of this kind was unimaginable."

"We must advance our plans with respect to the xhri space station."

"Should we not prioritize the first project and wait for the birth of the hol'la?"

"I fear the current situation does not permit waiting. The xhri and Ankhjaia'langtxhrl have lied to us. It is the only logical explanation. They informed us that the xhris, in spite of being sexed beings from the moment of their birth, voluntarily sterilize themselves in order to control the birth rate on their world. Now we know that is not true. If, when we decide to take the xhri base, we find that all of their abbas have been implanted, we will have no other course of action. We must do it now, before the xhris realize their reproductive capability and decide to use it for their own benefit."

"We must do it now," concurred another.

"Now." A third.

"Now," two voices said at the same time.

A few seconds passed. All eyes were fixed on Hithrolgh. "Now," he said at last.

MISUNDERSTANDINGS

Charlie was outside, on Xhroll's surface, taking a walk in woods of delicate slender trees whose silvery-gray, speckled white trunks reminded her of the birch trees surrounding her grandparents' house. It was an autumnal landscape in reds, ochres, and silvers spotted with the occasional greens. It was surprisingly warm, as if Nature was just starting its life cycle instead of approaching winter, like her mind was telling her. Small animals she recognized from prior walks and nicknamed "squirkeys"—squirrel monkeys seemed too long—were jumping from tree to tree overhead.

She still couldn't understand how, with such a sparse population and on such a beautiful planet, the Xhroll insisted on living underground, like moles, surrounded by plastic and metal. She would give anything to be able to spend the rest of her stay out in the fresh air, as she was doing now, the sun on her skin and the breeze tousling her hair. She sat down under a tree, her back leaning against the trunk, her gaze lost in the distant snow-frosted mountains, and felt a twinge of conscience for poor Nico, who would be facing his inexpressive therapist, answering repetitive, absurd questions.

She smiled to herself thinking about everything that had occurred during the last few hours. It seemed all her training in psychology was paying off. Nico was feeling better, that was obvious. And all because she had found a way to encourage his sense of self. And to shore up his masculinity which, in Nico's case, was the source of his every behavior.

She closed her eyes and let the gentle warmth of the sun on her skin bring back memories of Earth. Three years had gone by. Licia would have started college by now. The last message said she was thinking of majoring in underwater mining. Lars was going to devote a year to finding a permanent partner, and Michael was happy with his new spouse, although he missed her. After all, they'd been married for more than twelve years, and theirs had been a harmonious relationship that had come to a natural end from sheer wear and tear.

She also missed them all at times, during moments like these when the landscape favored reminiscing, because then the Earth's existence seemed credible. Unlike back at the base. At the base, she constantly had the impression that Earth must be some sort of collective hallucination, one shared by the whole crew of the *Victoria* so as to give some kind of meaning to their lives.

A low-pitched, sustained beep brought her back to reality. Having taken off her jumpsuit to get some sun, she searched its pockets until she found the location device she always carried along. Ankkhaia was trying to find her, but Charlie didn't at all feel like shutting herself back up inside the labyrinth of laminated corridors that was Xhroll's underworld, so she stopped the call and activated the tracking function. If Ankkhaia wanted to talk, let her come up and look for her.

Ankhjaia'langtxhrl saw the call light turn off and the tracking light turn on. If his manners had allowed for it, he would have kicked Nico's empty bed, as he'd seen him do when things didn't go as planned.

He made a quick mental calculation and calmed down a bit. Charlie wasn't very far away, just a fifteen-minute walk.

He didn't understand a thing. He hadn't found any information about Nico. He'd just disappeared, and the fact that his disappearance happened at the same time as Ankkhaia's meeting with Hithrolgh seemed ominous. It could be a coincidence, but for some time now every coincidence had turned out to have been orchestrated or planned by the xhreas.

In any case, something terrible must have happened for the abba to have disappeared without her ari-arkhj's knowledge. It couldn't be a premature birth; they would have informed both Charlie and himself. It must be something else, an even more serious matter than what he'd discussed with Hithrolgh. The problem was he couldn't figure out what it could be.

He went into one of the main ten-speed elevators and sat down on the seat closest to the door. He fastened the harness, grateful to be the only passenger in the vehicle, activated his journal, which he wrote in xhri, and began to review certain passages in an attempt to find a plausible answer to what was happening.

At times I find it almost laughable that our sociologists consider our society to be strongly dominated by the needs arising from the sex drive. Charlie laughed at that too, when I mentioned it to him. He says he cannot imagine an advanced society that's more sexually apathetic than ours, that not even their most primitive animals engage in sex as sparingly as we do. I tried to explain to him that our frequency rate cannot increase, given the small number of sexually active individuals on the planet, but she simply laughed and looked at me in a way I didn't recognize. That's the hardest thing about humans. To understand them, it's not enough to hear what they say. One would have to master many other codes, because they are all significant. They add to or subtract from the spoken word and, at times, even contradict it. He has explained to me that looks are loaded with meaning, and body movements are too: some are conscious and voluntary, others involuntary. How the body is positioned with respect to the conversation partner counts as well. As are social conventions, hierarchical differences, age, sex, skin color, the set of metaphysical beliefs known as religion, each individual speaker's memories and associations . . . It is dizzying. It is absolutely impossible for us to ever learn their language. Maybe we could establish a code clear enough to negotiate agreements or establish laws that bind the two peoples, but the whole human emotional and sentimental universe will forever be unavailable to us because it rarely expresses itself in linguistic terms. And we are not in the position, nor do I think we'll ever be, of interpreting meaning out of a blink or the angle of the lips in relation to the jaw or the nose.

Charlie, in turn, has the same complaint about us; that we are inscrutable, as he calls it. It seems humans feel as bothered about our own verbalization as we are about their constant gesture games.

I asked Charlie about his relationship with Nico and his other abbas. This is his third one, and only in legal terms. Charlie's two other hol'las are adult citizens already. One of them is a future abba, and the other one a future ari-arkhj. I find it strange to speak in these terms, but none of them has either implanted or been implanted, so that's why I have to accept they are what *he says they are, although in my own mental scheme they would both be xhreas if they are adults but haven't given life. I'm glad Charlie has done so. I would feel like I am taking something away from him by having implanted in his abba if it were the first time for Charlie.*

I am surprised that the xhreas haven't thought of the possibility of making Charlie try to implant in one of our abbas. It is also possible they haven't quite decided to impose on the xhris behaviors they clearly don't wish for themselves. I would like to think that's the reason.

The elevator reached its destination and Ankhjaia'langtxhrl turned the journal off, being no closer to clarity than he was before. Most of the information in it had been duly communicated to the departments in charge of archiving and channeling new data, but there was nothing there to justify that impossible violation of the rules on the part of the xhrea.

He finally located Charlie leaning against a tree. His clothes were tossed aside and he seemed to be enjoying the sun on his skin, his light brown skin covered with fine golden hairs shining in the light. Between his legs a triangle of hair similar to that on his head stood out. It immediately reminded Ankkhaia of Nico. She, Nico, had a patch just like that, but she also had hair over her chest, arms and legs. Not Charlie. Charlie was somewhere between himself and Nico.

Charlie opened his eyes when he saw Ankkhaia coming and showed all his teeth, as he always did, making that face of primal aggression Ankkhaia couldn't get used to, although he knew he must practice it to improve relations between the xhri and Xhroll. They liked it.

Ankkhaia sat next to Charlie and informed him of the situation in a succinct, precise manner, because there wasn't much to tell. Charlie sprang up and began pacing, five steps up, five steps back, slapping at the lower branches and mumbling to himself.

"I don't get it," he finally said, turning toward Ankhjaia'-langtxhrl.

"I don't either. Something unexpected must have come up. When was the last time you saw the abba?"

"Not even three hours ago."

"And how was she?"

Charlie shrugged.

"Ok, I'd swear. Happy. Satisfied."

"That's rare for the abba. It could be symptomatic of something."

Charlie smiled again

"This time it's normal. I gave a good boost to his macho ego."

"Can you explain that so I can understand?"

"I gave him what he wanted, what he needed."

"And what was that?"

Charlie gave a big snort. She always forgot that Ankkhaia wasn't a regular woman, even though she looked like one. Any regular woman would have understood her.

"Sex," she whispered. "You know."

Ankkhaia was staring at her, stone-faced.

"I went to bed with Nico. We made love. We had sexual intercourse. We copulated."

Ankkhaia sprung up like a jack-in-the-box and turned away. Charlie saw her handle something she held in her hands and for an anguished second was sure she was going to pull out a weapon and take her out right then and there, without further explanation. "My God," she thought. "How could I be such an idiot? She considers Nico her property. I have no idea if they have the concept of honor here, or how it works."

For a moment, she thought of fleeing through the forest and hiding somewhere until things cooled down, but it was only for a second. Clearly, that wasn't the solution. She had no recourse but to face up to whatever came her way.

Ankkhaia turned around slowly. Serene. Inexpressive. With empty hands.

"Now I understand," he said.

"So explain it to me, then."

Nico was curled up in bed, facing the door, trying not to totally lose consciousness, trying his best to keep himself awake enough to figure out what they were going to do with him. They had just given him an injection of something that was beginning to make him feel a sweet dizziness, a pleasant distancing from all his problems, even from himself. And he couldn't allow that. Not in the present circumstances.

He felt his eyes closing against his will, just as they did during the lectures on civic behavior at the Academy. Except that sleeping in class only resulted in a weekend detention, and here it could cost him his life. He tried to get up, but gave up immediately because his every muscle felt like rubber. He closed his eyes for a moment, trying hard to muster the strength to open them again a minute later.

When he managed to, the door was no longer located where it had been a few moments before and the walls were a different color. He closed his eyes again, feeling a sort of rocking motion, to and fro, as if he were lying in a hammock on the high seas. He reopened them, and the walls had turned black. There was also a light vibration in the air he was having trouble identifying. He shut his eyes and began sliding down a very long, very dark chute with a blood-red light at the end. The vibration intensified. "Ship," his brain said. "I am on a ship. We're going back home."

He'd spent too much time on space ships not to recognize that very subtle vibration you could hardly hear but could feel in your teeth, your testicles and in every bone in your body. What he couldn't understand was their taking him home. Why now? Why?

He pictured his question flowering into psychedelic colors, bursting into shiny wisps of smoke behind his closed eyelids, and he knew he'd lost the fight. They could do whatever they wanted with him. He wouldn't be conscious when it happened.

Ankhjaia'langtxhrl and Charlie were intercepted by a group of xhreas as they were returning underground.

The human assumed a fighting stance as she considered her possibilities: there were four xhreas. If she and Ankkhaia got the jump on them, they could finish them off in a couple of minutes. She took a quick look at Ankkhaia trying to signal her intentions as she indicated the two xhreas she meant to tackle. Ankkhaia looked back at her as cold as ever.

"What are you doing, Charlie?"

Charlie's heart fell into her boots.

"Fighting, of course. Can't you tell?"

"Fighting? What for?"

"What do you mean what for? Are you an idiot? I'm trying to survive."

"No one is going to make an attempt on your life. Is that really what you think of us? Xhroll never takes a life. It gives life."

The xhreas listened impassively to the conversation, conducted in xhri.

"We have to go with them. They will inform us shortly as to what's going on and what has been decided."

"How kind!"

Charlie would have liked to smash in any of those jerks' beautiful, calm faces but they and Ankkhaia had started walking toward the elevator and Charlie had no choice but to follow them. She could feel her blood boiling.

In perfect silence, they travelled the distance they had to cover, almost forty minutes by Charlie's watch, and during all that time no Xhroll moved one more muscle than was necessary for the ride. Charlie was just about ready to scream.

They finally reached a hall where six people awaited them: five men and one woman. Five xhreas and one ari-arkhj, Charlie corrected herself. They were all standing in a semicircle. It looked like some sort of war council and the six frigid stares didn't do much to ease the tension.

"Xhroll cannot allow what is going on," one of them said.

In the time she had spent among the Xhroll, Charlie had learned it was totally irrelevant to know who had spoken. When they began by saying 'Xhroll,' they spoke for everyone and their decision was final.

"Your visit has reached its end. We are now readying a ship to return you to your home base."

"Where is Nico?"

"In a safe place off-planet. You two will be reunited soon."

"Why have you taken him away without informing us?"

All questions came from Charlie, while Ankkhaia stared at the opposite wall with a look of either embarrassment or something else altogether.

"We are considering the possibility of performing the operation that would separate the hol'la from its abba's body right

143

away, but we still don't have any conclusive data about its level of development."

"Why the sudden rush?" Charlie was beginning to find the whole situation very suspicious.

"Your behavior has been grotesque and monstrous. Especially yours"—all eyes were on Charlie—"because the abba had no capacity to choose, you being its ari-arkhj."

"I am sorry to have offended you, but on our native planet that behavior is not only admissible but also desirable. It reinforces the psychic balance of the abba. What we don't think is right is to spy on the intimacy of two people who think they're alone."

The xhreas had no reaction whatsoever to the accusation and Charlie began to realize she was wasting her time. Whatever it was, the Xhrolls had already made up their minds.

"We understand your physiological needs are different from ours, and that's why we've come to the decision that before leaving you will have the chance to implant in one of our abbas. If viable, we will keep that hol'la and you will keep the one born from the human abba."

"What?" Charlie wavered between laughing hysterically and tearing fists first into whoever stood before her. "How am I going to . . .? That's completely absurd."

"Are you refusing to do it?"

Charlie had to make an effort to implement one of her diplomacy training's golden rules: always avoid answering "yes" or "no." But when you're asked if you refuse, it seems pretty stupid to answer "maybe."

"I'm not refusing," she said, taking a deep breath. "It's just that it isn't worth it. It wouldn't work."

"Why not?"

Something inside her wanted to yell: "Because I'm a woman, dumbass!" but during her time on Xhroll she'd started to acquire a sort of sixth sense around delicate subjects and had realized that, for her hosts, the topic of human sexuality was what weaponry was to Terrans: extremely interesting, but taboo; something you couldn't just ask about point blank. The Xhroll's entire social apparatus revolved around procreation and that's why they respected—and feared—those beings capable of conceiving. The deference shown to her from the beginning rested on their being convinced she was an ari-arkhj, a being capable of implanting life in an abba. If she now made it clear that if she were a member of Xhroll's society, she would possibly be an abba, although a non-implanted one, she would lose all her rights and they would very likely try to get her pregnant as soon as possible. If they couldn't—she was, after all, conveniently no longer fertile—she would become a simple xhrea, a neutered individual devoid of value to her hosts.

"It must have been some kind of mental block on my part," she finally said. "All right. I'll try it. And what if it doesn't work?"

Charlie thought she caught the xhreas exchanging significant looks, but she wasn't able to decipher them.

"Nothing. You will return home anyway."

Two of the xhreas who had escorted them there approached Charlie to accompany her out of the hall. Before she could utter a word, they answered her question:

"Ankhjaia'langtxhrl will join you later. After receiving instructions."

Nico woke up in an unfamiliar place, his head strangely clear and a gigantic erection bulging against the loose pants he wore for sleeping. As he caressed his swollen member, he ran his eyes around the room, trying to find out where he was before anyone realized he was awake. He was in a sort of sickbay, very similar to the one on the ship that had taken him to Xhroll. Everything was white and black, as always, and no other sound could be heard except for the usual vibration. And that wasn't a sound but a feeling.

Eyes closed, he concentrated on what his right hand was doing. Then he heard a faint noise of metal against glass. He sat up on his elbow searching the darkness for the source of the sound.

At the back of the room, inside a circle of light, a figure leaned over a workbench. The figure had a short black bob and, most unusually, was wearing some kind of white tunic that came up to mid-thigh, showing perfect legs. It was the closest he'd seen to a woman since they left the *Victoria*, not taking Charlie's naked body into account.

He got more comfortable and kept on looking at her. It could be anything, of course. What did anyone know when it came to the Xhroll? But to him she was a woman, a smallish, fragile woman, awfully feminine. From time to time she stepped to the right or to the left looking for some tool she needed, and Nico could admire the way she moved, as did his right hand in its own distinctive way.

He was beginning to really like that girl. It could be a fake girl, as Ankkhaia had turned out to be, but this time it wasn't a problem; everything that could go wrong for him already had. On that front there was no danger anymore.

The dark haired young woman got up on tiptoes to pick up a metal box from a shelf above her head and, as she did so, the gown she was wearing revealed for four or five seconds what he already knew but had forgotten: Xhrolls don't use any type of underwear.

He got up from his bed in feline silence and walked toward the back of the room, not having made a conscious decision but knowing in his guts that the young woman was going to pay in kind for his humiliation. He was going to screw her, no matter what.

It took him less than thirty seconds to throw himself on top of her, grab her in a chokehold with his left arm, use his own weight to force her down on the bench and use his right hand to help him penetrate her from behind. His belly was much more in the way than he would have wanted to admit, but there was nothing for it. Since he was already at it, he had to finish.

She'd tried to scream at first, but the pressure on her neck had made her give up right away. Now she didn't even struggle; she accepted his pounding with the same deadpan resignation with which those people did everything. He didn't care one way or the other. At that moment, the only thing that mattered to him was the feeling of being inside a woman's body; tight, hot, wet, the feeling he was in charge of his faculties, the feeling of being on the brink of exploding.

There was also pain, like the time before with Ankkhaia, but it was a bearable pain because it was him wanting it.

He looked in front of him and, on the polished metal surface covering the wall, he saw the woman's face: her eyes half closed, her mouth half open, her features distorted with pleasure, and he almost lost his rhythm. Those ice statues could feel! He was raping her and the chick liked it! For an instant the thought crossed his mind that her face could be registering pain, but he ignored that. Who cared.

He redoubled his efforts, totally forgetting his scruples, until he felt himself pouring into her in an endless tidal wave. Trying to stifle the noises coming out of him, short of breath, he collapsed on top of the woman's body. Her eyes were closed and she had just fainted.

He left her there on the bench and crawled back to his bed. It was possible they used hidden cameras, but for the moment he didn't care one bit; as long as he carried the bug inside him no one would dare touch a hair on his head, and afterward . . . time would tell.

Charlie was lying face down on her bunk on the ship, a bitter taste in her throat, like an onset of nausea that was taking too long. She hadn't felt that disgusted with herself for a long time. And she couldn't help but wonder why the disgust resulted from having lied to a Xhroll, when she'd spent half her life lying to male and female humans and had always found a reason to justify it. After all, it was her job, the one she'd been trained to perform, the only one she genuinely liked and had a real talent for.

Perhaps the disgust came from the fact that the poor abba was totally defenseless and innocent, outrageously innocent. The abba had simply looked at Charlie with wide-open eyes and begged her to grant her a life.

And she had pretended to try. Knowing that it was impossible. Knowing that for the Xhroll, copulating without hope of conception was an abomination. She had gone through the motions and gestures of making love to another body just like hers for the first time in her forty years. To save her own standing. Not even her own life, only her standing.

It was the first time she had seen an abba and, for a moment, she was bewildered. It hadn't occurred to her that the Xhroll wouldn't be physically different from each other, that they all had a vulva between their legs, which in human terms, made them all female. The only exception was that the ari-arkhjs had implanted breasts as a sign of rank or whatever it was, and the others did not.

She turned over roughly in bed. The entire mission had been a failure. She had learned nothing about the Xhroll that might be of value on Earth. Nico was a prisoner somewhere and hadn't even gotten rid of what he carried in his belly. Ank-khaia, who had almost become a friend, had turned cold as ice and refused to speak to her when she came aboard.

They would return to the base and then, what? Constant interrogations, hypnotic regressions, data verifications . . . and then, what? They were no closer to understanding the Xhroll now than before. And it was very likely that, after what had happened, the Xhroll would be eager to break off their minimal contact with the humans, those monsters who are fertile but sterilize themselves, who copulate during pregnancy, who think for themselves regardless of their sex and the best interests of their planet, who make gestures and faces and are in constant movement leading nowhere.

She punched her pillow a couple of times and changed position again. If Xhroll broke ties with Earth, she wouldn't be allowed to fly again. Naturally, a scapegoat would have to be found, and Nico wouldn't be enough.

And if, for any one of their strange reasons, the Xhroll decided to continue interacting with Earth, she would be expected to provide the necessary data to lay the groundwork for that relationship. What could Xhroll offer humans? What could humans provide in return? Charlie didn't know. She simply didn't know. The Xhroll were perfectly self-sufficient: they obtained every commodity they needed from several uninhabited planets; they had no luxuries of any kind; they didn't seem to have a wider aesthetic appreciation deriving from the contemplation of Nature; they fussed over their surface world the way an old-time English lord tended to his gardens, and that was that. Each one of them did their job well, and in their free time dedicated all their efforts to the enormous task of maintaining Nature. All their leisure time took place on the world outside: overseeing its ecological balance, repairing any damage caused by natural disasters, managing plagues and epidemics affecting the various plant and animal species, cutting down diseased trees, pruning others to create a beautiful natural landscape, transplanting some species, acclimating others. Theirs was a society of vocational gardeners, botanists, zoologists, environmental artists. It was the only thing that mattered to them, their only source of pleasure. As far as she knew, they didn't have fantasies, dreams, or ambitions. They were disgustingly dull.

And the worst of it: that was the only piece of information she could pass on to her superiors. Xhroll doesn't need us for anything; we don't need Xhroll for anything. There are no possibilities for commerce or any other type of exchange. We have found another intelligent species in the universe, but we have nothing to say to each other. Period.

They are so sharp that when we teach them our language they can infer hundreds of human social attitudes from our linguistic tropes. If a human being says "to arouse suspicion," a Xhroll understands that suspicion is always present in humans and it's just a matter of coming awake, since we earthlings don't ever trust anything or anyone. If you explain to them that there is also the phrase "to conceive a suspicion," it's much worse, because we use the same verb for suspicion as for the beginning of life. This implies that we assign a positive value to the birth of a suspicion about someone. Beautiful, right?

We can try to pass our vices and our sense of fun on to them, they can give us their asceticism and lack of humor, their work ethic, their concept of obedience. But is that what we want?

She turned over in bed again and decided to sleep no matter what. Those weren't her problems, after all. Earth was full of experts whose job was to look for solutions. That's why they got paid. She closed her eyes tight, like she used to when she was a little girl, clenched her fists, and applied herself as best she could to the task of falling asleep.

LIFE MISSION

Commander Kaminsky looked at the officers of his General Staff, his expression at its sourest, and without even taking time to greet them got straight to the point:

"Ladies and gentlemen, the Xhroll have mobilized."

The officers exchanged worried, confused glances.

"Captain Fonseca has just sent a signal saying that they are outside of Xhroll space and heading toward us. We have no way of knowing if something unusual has happened, or if it's all over and they're just returning our officers to us as planned."

"Isn't it too soon, commander?" a voice called out.

"According to our numbers it's at least one month too soon, but our human calculations may not necessarily apply in this case. It's possible that everything is fine." He paused as if unsure just how far to take his suspicions. "But it's also possible that's not the case. Therefore, I've decided to have weapons ready in the event we have to repel an attack. If anyone's got anything to say, say it now."

"Commander." Colonel Ortega had risen to her feet. "Isn't this a bit drastic, seeing as we have no information about their intentions?"

"I said I want weapons ready, Colonel, not that I'm going to use them. I don't think it's a good idea to risk the survival of the *Victoria* by being overly naive. Once the Xhroll ship has contacted us we will request the necessary information, but I am not going to wait for them to shoot first."

"Then we will?"

"I hope that won't be necessary, but I wanted to inform you all so that you could pass on whatever information you think necessary to your subordinates. While the idea isn't to generate mass hysteria, everyone should be clear that our friendship with the Xhroll is very superficial and may well be based on misunderstandings on both sides. I want all personnel on the *Victoria* to be aware of that and to be in a constant state of alert. And if my suspicions are wrong and the Xhroll come as peaceful visitors to return our officers, we'll accord them the appropriate honors. However, all types of nonpublic fraternization with their women are expressly forbidden. Have I made myself clear?"

"You can chat, you can drink, but no screwing," summarized Colonel Nátchez, his eyes glued to the ceiling and his voice as emotionless as a conference translator.

The officers exchanged discreet smiles.

"Exactly." The commander looked like someone who suffered from chronic indigestion.

"Same goes for our women with their men, Commander?"

"I said all types, Colonel Ortega."

"In that case, you mean fraternization with their women and men, Commander."

Kaminsky stared at Diana Ortega for several long seconds, but she refused to lower her gaze.

"If I'm forced to declare a state of emergency," he said in

a low, strangled voice, "you'll have to get over these linguistic concerns, Colonel, *sir*."

"Yes sir. Pardon me, sir."

"Meeting adjourned. Everyone to their posts. Level three alert."

Ankhjaia'langtxhrl was in a room with some two hundred other ari-arkhjs, waiting to be joined by whoever the Xhroll had put in charge of the special mission they'd been sent on. For the first time ever, Ankhjaia'langtxhrl was taking part in an operation where everyone present was of the same sex, and the situation felt strange and terribly unnerving. Neither the xhreas nor the abbas would have been able to understand that feeling of discomfort because living all together was the norm for them, and the presence of ari-arkhjs, the exception. For the latter group, however, this was something unfamiliar.

He gazed at the faces of the others, clearly sensing that they shared his inner trembling. There was complete silence, complete stillness. Ankhjaia'langtxhrl closed his eyes as the only way to distance himself from the others. He opened them shortly afterward upon realizing that the arkhj, the one put in charge, had just arrived.

If Ankhjaia'langtxhrl were human he probably would have leapt to his feet, eyes and mouth wide open, just like he had seen Charlie do so many times when something had astonished him. As he was Xhroll, he merely stared fixedly at Hithrolgh, who had just brought the group's wait to an end.

"You have been briefed on our mission's purpose. This is the first time in the history of Xhroll that a ship is full of ari-arkhjs, with the minimum number of xhreas necessary for ship maintenance and only one abba aboard: the xhri abba that soon will give us a life. We have almost no information about the xhris' motivations and customs, but Ankhjaia'langtxhrl will share what little we know before we make contact with them. You are well aware of the importance of our mission: the very survival of Xhroll depends on it.

"This is also the first time in our modern history that Xhroll will commit an act of violence against another world, albeit an act of relative violence."

"One cannot use violence when copulating. It is absolutely impossible," said one of those present.

Hithrolgh was silent for a few seconds.

"One can," he finally said. "It is monstrous, but possible. For the good of Xhroll. Ankhjaia'langtxhrl," he continued, "you have had time to think about the best way of achieving our goal. Speak."

Hithrolgh was right. Ankkhaia had had time to think about it. What he had never had was the desire to do so. He couldn't accept that violence was necessary, not even for the good of Xhroll. He was aware that in three or four generations the Xhroll would become extinct unless they found a way to restore their genetic potential, damaged so long ago, or encountered a compatible species willing to contribute to their survival. But being aware of the problem did not give him the right to employ a solution that went against all the norms of conduct that the Xhroll had created and upheld—until the xhrea had decided to change them. Yet it was a decision made by and for Xhroll, and it wasn't his job to question any solution that could lead to the survival of his people. His job was to provide information and, by doing so, contribute to their success, and to life.

"The xhri are not like us," he began. "They don't have xhrea. Or they do, in that everyone voluntarily becomes xhrea. They can all reproduce if they wish, but because of that their population is so large they voluntarily deny themselves the chance to reproduce in order to limit their numbers. An opposite problem to ours."

"We are able to implant in their abbas, if we can generalize from the one known case. Similarly, we believe their ari-arkhjs cannot implant in a Xhroll abba. The experiment was tried, but it failed. That's why all aboard this ship are ari-arkhjs. Our mission is to select xhri abbas and try to implant in them all."

"The xhri abbas' bodies are similar to those of our abbas and xhreas, with two visible exceptions: they have a large amount of hair attached to the skin, and an appendage in the sexual area that we are able to insert comfortably in our genitalia, although there is some pain, I think for the abba as well.

"While copulating, the xhris move constantly. Their movements are spasmodic and painful and they frequently cry out. They breathe noisily and become covered with a body fluid excreted through the skin.

"The also emit a viscous fluid through the appendage in the sex area that Ankhjaia'langtxhrl mentioned earlier," added Hithrolgh.

"True. How do you know that, Hithrolgh?"

"I am a physician."

Ankhjaia'langtxhrl might have wanted to ask something else, but did not. He continued:

"In my experience, they do not think at all about the life that copulation represents, because copulation for them is always sterile. I believe it best not to mention procreation at all."

"You all are not to speak with them. Talking with the xhri causes mental confusion. You are going to implant life."

"But if they do not want to be implanted, how will we do it? They are not going to allow us. We cannot restrain them by force."

Hithrolgh put his hand in his pocket and withdrew a tiny ampoule that he showed to those present.

"We will drug them with this compound. It can be mixed in a drink or injected. It lasts long enough for you to complete your mission."

"And what about their xhreas, or their ari-arkhjs? Will they allow it? According to the linguistic analyses, the xhri are a violent species."

"They will all be drugged except the abbas, who will be confined in our ship's cargo hold until they decide to cooperate and we reach an agreement."

The ari-arkhjs' rigid posture left no doubt as to their opinion of the plan; the look in their eyes, however, made clear that they would follow it through to the end. Hithrolgh relaxed inside. After what had been happening on Xhroll lately, it was just this side of possible the ari-arkhjs would have refused to obey his orders.

"Hithrolgh, I want to speak with you." Ankhjaia'langtxhrl came over to him when the session had ended.

"I do not, Ankhjaia'langtxhrl."

Hithrolgh turned away and was lost in the darkness of the hallway.

For a moment, when she saw Ankkhaia silhouetted against the outer blackness, Charlie had a strong feeling of déjà vu, as if time had frozen and they were still aboard the ship that was taking them to Xhroll.

Charlie spared herself the pointless greeting and stood up to talk, Xhroll-style. Ankkhaia entered the cubicle, showed all her teeth, said "Hello, Charlie," and sat down on the bunk. Charlie made an exasperated face, gave a short laugh that even to her sounded like a bark, and sat next to Ankkhaia.

"Do you have some way of contacting your base, Charlie?"

For a moment Charlie couldn't move. Clearly they had captured the signal she had just sent; they'd barely completed a jump and now wanted to know if she planned to deny it.

She knew Ankkhaia could not yet read her facial expressions; nevertheless, she got up from the bunk and turned to face the wall.

"What's wrong?" *Ask another question, buy some time, think.*

"You must try to communicate with them. Something terrible is going to happen."

"Is Xhroll going to attack us?"

"Yes."

"Because of what happened between Nico and me?"

"No. Because Xhroll needs lives."

An image popped into her head of Xhrolls like vampires from old-time movies: dressed all in black, impassive, cold. Draining the humans' lifeblood, killing them in order to give life to Xhroll.

"Are you going to kill us?"

"Is this a personal obsession, or is it something common to all xhri?"

"What?"

"That stubborn belief that we want to kill you."

"I don't understand you, Ankkhaia."

"The xhreas have brought us here. Two hundred ari-arkhjs, almost all of us there are, so that we can implant in your abbas whether they want to or not."

"What for?" Charlie thought as fast as she could, without coming up with anything.

"I just told you. To give lives to Xhroll."

"That's ridiculous. There can't be more than seventy-three women on board. Even supposing all of them got pregnant, that's a ridiculously small number for an entire planet."

"Your abbas will be kept constantly implanted until the end of their lives. There are more than two hundred abbas on the base. In twenty or thirty years that means almost five thousand lives. Do you understand?"

"But you're talking about men. On the base there are more than two hundred men, yes. Are you going to rape the men?"

"Rape?"

"Copulate by force, against the will of one of the participants."

For the first time since they'd met, Ankkhaia seemed genuinely horrified.

"You have a word for that aberration?"

Charlie bit her lower lip, wishing she could take back the words she'd just said.

"Yes."

"Then, you humans do it, too?"

"It's an obsolete word, ancient. It happened on occasion, like during wartime to humiliate the enemy. It hasn't happened in centuries," she lied.

"To humiliate, not to give life," Ankkhaia said in a low voice, trying to understand that concept, one of the first she had come across without ever being able to grasp.

Suddenly, Charlie realized what Ankkhaia was trying to tell her.

"You're going to rape our MEN?"

Ankkhaia's tone of voice raised imperceptibly.

"Your abbas! Those among you who are able to conceive, whatever they're called."

Charlie started to laugh, and the more she thought about it, the more hysterical her laughter became. She threw herself on the bed and began punching the canvas-like cloth that served as a mattress. Ankkhaia watched her with such a dumbfounded expression that Charlie's laughter intensified instead of subsiding. She couldn't help it. Every time she pictured the scene she had a fit of laughter. The men of the *Victoria* running in terror through the corridors while the Xhroll girls, with their dyed eyes and fake hair, pursued them relentlessly, their expressions calm and icy, and when they caught the men they ripped off their pants and mounted them by force while the men cried and begged for help.

She couldn't explain why it was so funny. It if had been the other way around it would have seemed horrifying, but she couldn't help it. She knew she should use every ounce of strength to prevent such a thing from happening and yet, in some corner of her mind, a sharp, age-old voice laughed roughly, saying, *Let it happen, Charlie. What's it to you? For once, you're safe precisely because you're a woman. Let them rape those macho men. It's a fraction of what they have coming to them for the thousands of years of pain and humiliation we women have suffered. This alone could do more for sexual equality than all the pretty words that have been spoken in the last three centuries. Let them suffer firsthand what we've suffered all through history. For once let them be the ones who cry, who go crazy with terror and disgust, who must lower their eyes when asking for justice.*

"Charlie," urged Ankkhaia, "can you contact your base?"

"What do they plan to do with our ari-arkhjs?"

"Imprison you until you cooperate."

"What kind of cooperation?"

"Until you grant us the right to protect your abbas and continue implanting in them."

"We don't have that right. On Earth, everyone decides for themselves."

"That leads to collective disaster."

"Very possibly," Charlie said nonchalantly.

She couldn't stop thinking about how fun it would be to see Kaminsky crying through the hallways after being raped by one of those amazons who wore fake, implanted breasts to mark their reproductive capacities. And the chaplain? Would they do him the honor of elevating him to the sacred rank of mother? That would certainly be something to report to the Holy See.

It would be fun, sure, but its price would be war. The first transsolar war in human history, and that would definitely be less fun. It was doubtful that the Central Government would really retaliate for the rape of seventy female officers, but if it was a matter of the "abominable humiliation"—she could just hear the words—of two hundred male members of the Central Government Fleet, that would be different. So what if there were five women in the Central Government? They were five against twenty. Earth would retaliate. And no one knew what Xhroll had in its arsenal to counter human weapons. One thing was clear: they moved through space faster and better than humans did. It wouldn't take them long to reach the edge of Earth's solar system, and then their actions couldn't be foreseen. She supposed they wouldn't be violent, because the Xhroll didn't kill. But then again, she had also thought them incapable of rape.

"Charlie, we don't have much time."

"I know, I know. Please leave. I've got to think."

Ankkhaia looked at her for a few seconds, then rose and left in silence.

An alarm lit up on the console where he was working. Hithrolgh sat looking at it for a moment, as if not understanding its meaning. Then it took a few more seconds to shake off the thoughts overtaking him. The news he had just received was so unprecedented, so devastating, that he hadn't yet been able to react.

And now that same alarm was telling him that the abba must be operated on immediately because the hol'la had finished growing and it was time to bring it into the world.

Almost automatically, he issued a summons for all members of the medical team that would be needed for the operation, and then he held his hands out in front of him to see if they were shaking. Only another Xhroll with similar medical training would have noticed his inner trembling; to any observer's eye, his pulse was perfectly steady. But Hithrolgh knew that wasn't true, that the risk of error was too high.

He massaged a calming agent into both wrists and took several slow, deep breaths trying to clear his mind, getting ready for the greatest responsibility Xhroll had ever faced. Some time back the decision not to use the surgical bot had been made. They couldn't let a machine programmed to operate on a Xhroll body be in charge during surgery on a xhri. It required a thinking being, a being capable of making quick decisions based not only on logic but on intuition and the needs of the moment.

He had spent months studying the reports on the hol'la's development, the diagrams that showed the structure and function of the xhri body, its response to different kinds of anesthesia. But the responsibility was enormous, with no guarantee of success.

Hithrolgh tapped two other call codes into his terminal: Ankhjaia'langtxhrl and the xhri ari-arkhj should be present, although he didn't like the idea. Some of Xhroll's norms had had to be changed for the planet's survival, but that was no excuse for flouting all of them for reasons of personal preference.

He slowly removed his wig while thinking about Ankhjaia'langtxhrl. It seemed incredible to him that some corner of his brain was still able to remember the feel of his skin, considering that they had not really touched each other again since that long-ago moment when it had become clear that Hithrolgh was a xhrea and, therefore, unable to give life. For a while the two had thought procreation would be possible, if they truly wanted it. They were so young. So very inexperienced. They still knew how to dream.

Now they both had the survival of Xhroll in their hands, but they were not together. Never again would they be. Or maybe they would. Just maybe . . .

The second alarm sounded when Hithrolgh was already at the door. He ignored it and headed quickly to the operating room for sterilization. The others were already prepped and waiting around the slab where the abba, eyes dilated and skin almost gray, was shouting incomprehensibly in his native language. The other xhri answered in a low, gentle voice, probably trying to calm him down.

Hithrolgh entered the operating room covered in sealing fluid, as were the others. If the procedure lasted more than two hours, they would have to set up shifts so each could exit and break the seal and in that way let their skin breathe. But maybe that would be unnecessary.

His eyes met Ankhjaia'langtxhrl's; then his gaze turned to the abba who was making a strange sound by knocking top and bottom teeth together and whose eyes were starting out of their sockets. One look at the monitor showed that the xhri's heart was pounding at an alarming rate.

"Tell me what you're gonna do to me! Tell me!" the xhri shouted raggedly, accented speech making the words almost unintelligible. One of Hithrolgh's assistants placed a tiny device in the abba's ear and activated the translator, programmed with all the data that Ankhjaia'langtxhrl and Charlie had entered during hundreds of work sessions.

"We are going to give you an anesthetic that will be injected between two spinal vertebrae. It is painful, but over quickly. Anesthesia is considered the best option for preventing harm to the hol'la, and we have no way of knowing what level of pain you will have to endure. We believe the surgery will take less than forty minutes. You will wear an oxygen mask. Breathe slowly and deeply. Think about life. Xhroll matters. You do not."

"Easy, Nico, take it easy," Charlie interjected, "that's just a thing they say. It helps them. Of course you matter. We won't let anything happen to you."

Nico tried desperately to grab hold of Charlie's hand, but the xhrea completely surrounded him and all he could see of her were her eyes, looking out at him from between the aliens' shoulders.

Ankkhaia stood next to him.

"Grab hold of my neck, Nico. This is going to hurt."

He did what was asked and his howls of pain echoed through the room while they administered the shot in his back.

Then, little by little, the pain subsided. He lay back down in spite of the catheter and they tied his hands to the slab. Then he closed his eyes for an instant, and when he opened them again all he saw was a landscape of crystalline eyes and silvery faces through the sterilization fluid.

He lifted his gaze to the ceiling, where they had installed some kind of VR screen that displayed an abstract painting. He concentrated on it, trying to forget his real circumstances. He saw how a red line appeared in the artwork that grew wider by the second, while in the center something moving and whitish in color appeared.

Suddenly, something made him roar like a wounded beast. It was a hammering pain, a savage rhythm that ran the length of his body and got faster and hotter, as if they were ripping his guts out. His whole body convulsed to the beat of those unyielding contractions. He began to scream.

"Hang in there, Nico!" He heard Charlie's voice. "It's almost over. Watch the screen. Your son or daughter is being born."

And then he realized that what he had taken to be a VR screen was some kind of monitor that let him follow what was going on at the level of his groin, and that the red line was actually the enormous gash they had cut in him to extract the creature, and that the white thing was . . . had to be . . .

He fainted. They immediately revived him with oxygen and slaps on the cheeks. His mouth filled with hot, bitter vomit and they brought over a bowl for him to throw up into. The pain was unbearable.

Then someone yanked at his intestines, like the priest of some ancient cult that rips out their victims' beating hearts, and everyone in the room exhaled together, a short, quick expulsion of breath that could be heard above his final howl of pain.

Someone injected a different liquid into the infusion pump hanging at neck level and the pain began to diminish.

"It's here, Nico! It's here!" Charlie's voice sounded hysterically happy. He couldn't remember what was happening.

"It's a beautiful baby, Nico! Looks like everything turned out fine. Yep, all fine!"

At that point, Nico realized she was speaking to him and what she was talking about.

"Is it a boy or girl?" he heard Charlie ask. He didn't care. The only thing he wanted was to be left in peace, for them to be done with him and leave him to sleep, taking the creature with them.

Ankkhaia looked up from the baby, and in spite of his eternally expressionless face his eyes were shining with happiness.

"It is a living being, healthy and strong. You will have to wait until almost fifteen of your years to know its sex. But that does not matter. It does not matter."

He lowered his eyes again, lost in thoughtful contemplation of that little bundle of crying rose-colored flesh.

Charlie hurried into Nico's cubicle and found Hithrolgh, Ankkhaia, and some other xhrea surrounding the bed. Nico was practically sitting upright. He was sucking on a soft bottle and looking from one Xhroll to another, his expression that of a spoiled child who has chosen to disobey, come what may.

"Hey, what the hell is going on?"

"The abba refuses to feed the hol'la."

"He what?" yelled Charlie.

"I am not a goddamn cow. My mission is over."

"Your mission is over when I say it is. That little girl is a human baby boy or girl, a female or male citizen of Earth, and we are not going to put her or his life on the line because you refuse to cooperate."

"That little girl isn't even a girl. Even they don't know what it is. And it's none of my business. Let 'em give it powdered milk if they want."

"Is that possible?" Charlie asked Hithrolgh.

"Unfortunately, it is not. In two days that will be fine, but for the first fifty-four hours after birth it is essential that the hol'la be nourished by the abba's body fluid. The hol'la's digestive system is not yet developed enough to absorb any other type of nutrients."

"There, you heard."

Nico shook his head slowly, defiantly.

"That's an order, Lieutenant Andrade."

He smiled.

"Aw, Charlie, get real! After you told me your life story, complete with intimate details? After you opened your legs for me of your own free will, after all that you're giving me orders?"

Charlie went pale.

"That is an order!"

He smiled again.

"And what are you going to do if I refuse? Hit me?" He looked around. "They won't let you. I'm an abba of Xhroll."

"You're a stinking piece of shit."

Charlie unholstered a small, late-model plastic gun and rested it with a perfectly steady hand against Nico's temple.

"You are going to nurse that baby or I'll blow your brains out, Andrade."

His face drained of color.

"You wouldn't."

"But first I'll shoot your dick off, since apparently that's what you care about most. Yeah, let's start there."

Charlie walked slowly around to the foot of the bed, yanked the sheets off, and pointed the gun between Nico's legs.

The Xhroll watched the scene without expression, remote.

"Aren't you fucking sons of bitches going to do anything? This psycho wants to kill me."

"You want to kill the hol'la," Ankkhaia said with perfect calm.

"Well, Andrade? What's your decision?"

Nico hurled the bottle against the wall, which silently absorbed it.

"Fine! Fine, dammit! Have them bring it here!"

Two xhrea quickly left the cubicle and returned a few minutes later with the crying baby.

Hithrolgh helped the xhri uncover his chest and fit the tiny mouth to the flat nipple. The infant began to suck and the tension in the room relaxed.

"Leave us alone," Charlie asked.

When everyone else had left the room, she sat down on the bed, pistol still in hand, and looked at the baby as it sucked away, focused on that alone, its eyes closed and its hands clenched into tiny fists. Nico held it with seeming disgust and avoided looking at it.

"Happy?" he asked at last.

"For now, yes."

There was a long silence, the only sound being the baby's sucking, punctuated by short pauses.

"Would you have done it, Charlie?"

She looked him directly in the eye, not blinking.

"Yes."

Nico swallowed.

"In fact, I'm still thinking of doing it. In fifty hours you'll no longer be needed. Not by him or her, not by the Xhroll, not by the humans. Move its nose away from your chest! It needs to breathe while it nurses."

"I guess it's true you had a child."

"Of course it's true."

"When you told me the story it sounded so theatrical . . ."

"Because that *was* theater: a trick I learned in psychology classes. No one ever raped me and my decision to go into Space Intelligence was totally my own. But it is true that I have kids. Two. All grown up now."

There was another long silence. The baby stopped sucking and fell asleep nestled against Nico's chest.

"Charlie, tell me the truth. Did they send you here to kill me?"

She raised the gun, pointed it for a second at Nico's fore-head, turned it toward the wall as if playing. Then she put it back in her holster.

It made no sense for him to know that he was worth even less to the humans than he was to the Xhroll, that her orders included getting him out of the way, discretely or openly, if circumstances required it. No need for Nico to know that. Not now that everything had turned out well and they were heading home. Knowing Nico and his all too predictable lack of perspective, if she'd had answered yes, within a few hours the whole world would be accusing the Central Government of murder.

"No," she said at last. "But you never know, do you?"

She gathered the baby up with infinite care and left the cubicle without saying goodbye.

GREAT EXPECTATIONS

Hithrolgh and Ankhjaia'langtxhrl were having lunch together in the empty sickbay. In the next room the hol'la was sound asleep after having been fed.

They both sat staring into their bowls, and the silence between them had a gelatinous quality to it. Ankhjaia'langtxhrl spoke first.

"Is there any doubt that your surgery assistant has become implanted?"

"None."

"But he's a xhrea."

"Yes. That's what's so incredible. And by an abba . . ."

"A xhri abba."

"And without being a willing participant . . ."

"That's what we were going to do to them. It doesn't matter anymore. It is a life for Xhroll."

"Now we are really at the mercy of the xhri, Ankhjaia'langtxhrl. Now it is foolish to think of taking their abbas from the base in order to get five thousand lives when, if we can consistently replicate what happened with my assistant, the xhri abbas could implant all our xhrea. It would save us."

"From what I know of humans, and I know it isn't much, we would have to pay them for it."

"And what could they want from us?"

"That's the bitter pill, Hithrolgh. We have nothing they could want in return."

"Nothing? Not even information or raw materials?"

"They are interested mainly in means of destruction, Hithrolgh, and we don't have any. Our technological development is at about the same level as theirs, and so is our science. We don't have any art, what they call art." And, catching Hithrolgh's look of incomprehension: "Useless things with no practical value that, according to their subjective evaluation, are beautiful."

"Like a dark lake glimmering at sunrise?"

"Yes, but manufactured, not natural."

"I understand."

Both of them resumed eating without enthusiasm, lost in thought. Suddenly Ankhjaia'langtxhrl got up.

"Wait for me here. I'm going to look for Charlie."

"You cannot inform that xhri of something that's crucial for our survival. I haven't even informed Xhroll yet. If I've told you, it's because I need you to help me think. There are no other xhrea here and you have a good mind."

Ankhjaia'langtxhrl stood in the doorway.

"Charlie also has a quick mind, knows his people, loves life. He will be willing to help us."

Hithrolgh lowered his head and Ankhjaia'langtxhrl left. Almost inadvertently, he held his hands over his belly hoping, wanting. The news had been devastating in terms of its potential for hope and frustration. If the xhrea could be implanted, Xhroll would survive. It would survive forever and ever. And the xhrea wouldn't have to depend exclusively on the abbas and the ari-arkhjs. They could be equal, as they used to be in the olden days.

The thought of carrying a hol'la inside him crossed Hith-rolgh's mind for a second, and he trembled with longing. But that would mean they would depend on the xhri, who could ask any price in exchange for giving them life. A price that, accord-ing to Ankhjaia'langtxhrl, they wouldn't be able to pay.

Charlie walked nimbly into sickbay, all her teeth bare.

"Congratulations, Hithrolgh. Ankkhaia told me everything. I'm really very happy for you."

"Do you think the humans will cooperate?"

"Yes, they will. But using volunteers only, and they will ask a high price."

"What can we give you?"

Charlie scratched her head.

"I've thought about it, and I know the only thing our Gov-ernment will be interested in is land, physical space capable of sustaining human life. A section of Xhroll world's crust on which to establish a human colony. It's a dream held by generations: a genuine colony on a genuinely habitable world."

The two Xhroll remained still, frozen to the spot.

"That's impossible," said Hithrolgh.

"I thought as much. It would be like letting a biker gang set up camp in the gardens of Versailles."

"I don't understand."

"It doesn't matter. I mean, it's unacceptable."

"What about if they only stayed temporarily? They could enjoy Xhroll during the time it takes for the hol'la to grow inside their respective abbas."

"A seven- or eight-month-long idyllic vacation offered by Xhroll to those humans who would like to come over and act as studs," muttered Charlie to herself. "No."

"Why not?

"Because it would be unconstitutional: it wouldn't be gender-equal. And besides, we haven't fought for centuries and achieved our current legal and even linguistic equal rights so that our planet's males can go back to thinking they are the masters of creation spurred on by your reverence for reproductive power. No way."

"I don't understand that, Charlie."

"It doesn't matter. It's quite complicated and you lack data. You just have to realize that those volunteering for such a deal wouldn't quite be the best, or the most peaceful, or the most respectful among us. They would be like Nico, or even worse. And they would all be running around your planet, a paradise, destroying things for fun or because they're bored, littering, altering the natural balance, raping your female . . . your male xhreas, your abbas, and your ari-arkhjs, humans don't see much of a difference . . . It would be a free brothel."

"A what?"

"Forget it."

Charlie bit her lower lip. She had the impression that her feelings had carried her too far. She had just given her hosts the impression that all humans, and especially male humans, were scum, some kind of rampaging monsters one had to keep at bay. And that—besides being personally abhorrent to her because it was neither true nor nuanced enough—went totally against her orders. What she should have tried to do was exactly the opposite: convince them that humans, in general, were kind, peaceful, and cooperative; try to establish the basis for

unprejudiced dialogue that would lead to the settlement of a
human colony on Xhroll and encourage Xhroll visits to Earth.
All of that sounded so good on paper but came crashing down
in ruins as soon as she pictured a unit of three or four thousand
young men on board the Fleet's ships on their way to a planet
where they'd not only be able to give free rein to their sexual
desires, they'd be appreciated for it.

And it was a disservice to human women, who had finally
managed to liberate themselves to a great extent from mental
enslavement based on their reproductive functions.

"Hithrolgh, would you leave us alone for a moment? There's
something I'd like to discuss with Ankkhaia."

"I am the spokesperson for my world."

"It's something personal, between ari-arkhjs. Between ari-
arkhjs sharing the same abba," she added, using absurd logic in
an attempt to strengthen her request.

Without another word, Hithrolgh crossed over to the next
cubicle where the hol'la was sleeping, totally oblivious to the
fact that two worlds' futures were being debated next to its crib.

Charlie turned toward Ankhjaia'langtxhrl, her mind running at full speed.

"Ankkhaia, has the implantation of an adult xhrea by an ari-
arkhj ever been tried?"

"You mean after the trial period?"

"Yes, between fully developed individuals."

"We reach our sexual peak at approximately fifteen of your
years. At that point, we try it. If it doesn't work, we get classified for life. Making other attempts after that point would be
abhorrent. The xhrea would never allow it. They would feel . . ."
Ankkhaia seemed at a loss for words.

"Humiliated?"

"Maybe. Used in an improper manner. I cannot quite visualize the concept and I have no words for it."

"Do you think Hithrolgh would be willing to try it with you?"

"No."

"Why not?"

"Why would he have to?"

"Because there's a chance, granted a remote one, that many of you don't reach sexual maturity until much later than the statutory age. If that xhrea was able to become implanted by Nico, maybe you would be capable of implanting Hithrolgh."

Ankkhaia stared into the void for two whole minutes by Charlie's watch.

"No," he finally answered.

"Why not? You two have known each other a long time, you're both here alone, I mean, if it doesn't work, Xhroll wouldn't have to find out. It's your survival as a species and your liberation from us that's at stake. If it works, you won't need us for anything; your future will be yours alone. You have nothing to lose."

"It's impossible, Charlie. Xhreas cannot conceive. They just can't."

"Why is that?"

"Because they are xhrea."

"That's just semantics."

"Reflecting reality."

"Or imposing it and not allowing any of you to think differently."

Ankhjaia'langtxhrl remained deep in thought for a while.

"Would you try to implant a dead body?"

"The crazy ideas you come up with, Ankkhaia! Of course not."

"And why is that?"

"Because it's impossible. Because a dead body . . ."

Charlie suddenly stopped when she understood Ankh-jaia'langtxhrl's line of reasoning.

"But now you have proof that it may work, despite the mental block caused by your truism, Ankkhaia! Don't you see? Since Nico didn't know any better, he imposed no barriers on himself and went for it. And it worked! It could work for you and Hithrolgh too, and for thousands of others."

"Even if it did work, our whole society would change. If things turn out as you think, many xhrea might become not only abba but also ari-arkhj. It's even possible that the xhrea, the third element of our society, will become extinct. The consequences are immeasurable."

"The alternative is either extinction or dependence on a xhri species who will make you pay for each new life."

Ankkhaia fell silent once again. Then, finally, he rose very slowly to his feet.

"Xhroll comes first. I will speak to Hithrolgh."

BEGINNINGS

Nico, ensconced in an armchair in Olympia Hall amid a sea of people, looked like a medieval king receiving tribute from his vassals.

They'd hurried to find him a uniform three sizes larger than what he usually wore so as to hide as much as possible the fat he'd put on over the last few months. And although his cheeks were chubbier and his belly softer and more pronounced than he would have liked for his first public appearance, his recently trimmed moustache and cocky smile gave him the "Nico Andrade" air they all knew so well.

The official ceremony had ended a few minutes earlier, and while the High Command was meeting with the representatives from Xhroll, Nico installed himself triumphantly in Olympia Hall to regale his friends and colleagues with his adventures.

He'd been warned from the start that he was only allowed to talk about events directly related to his own personal experience until it was decided what information could be made public. But when Charlie showed up after several hours of official conversations, Nico, by then fairly drunk, was describing what sounded more like Alice's adventures in Wonderland.

"The babes, oh man, the babes! Like the ones you see here, only better. And all of them waiting on me hand and foot, taking care of my every need. Whatever I wanted I got on a silver platter."

Charlie smiled wryly and went over to one of the coffee machines. She helped herself to a cup and, warming her hands with it, joined the small group of diehards still gathered around Nico. The rest had gotten tired and gradually drifted off.

Charlie leaned discreetly against one of the metal columns, partially hidden from the eyes of Nico's open-mouthed audience. She listened in silence.

"But I screwed one of them," he was saying, his words sounding increasingly slurred. "Just picture it, me just about ready for the bug to pop out, my gut as big as the Earth. The idiot Xhroll, probably convinced that in my condition I wasn't a danger to anyone, starts doing experiments in the lab right there in my room. Wearing a short dress and no undies."

Laughter punctuated Andrade's story.

"What can I say, guys? I screwed her. Just like that. With any luck, now she's the one carrying a bug inside of her."

He couldn't continue, there was so much laughter.

"No, Nico." All eyes turned toward her. A few made weak attempts at a salute, which Charlie cut off with a gesture. "That woman you screwed, as you yourself just said, can't have gotten pregnant because she's not a woman. You realize that, right?" Charlie had spent so much time preparing the lies, looking for the right moment to launch them, that the first one issued forth smooth and natural, perfectly believable, just like always.

"What?" His brow was damp with sweat and his cheeks were flushed. "I should know, I'm the one who stuck it in her."

"You also stuck it in the other one and look what happened."

Eyes went from Charlie to Nico like in a tennis match.

"Your problem, Nico, is that you insist on not seeing reality even when it's right in front of you. The hell with in front, not even when you're right inside of it."

"What reality?" His voice shook. He would have given anything to make Charlie Fonseca shut up.

"The woman you so proudly screwed is a man, Lieutenant Andrade. So is the other one, the one who made you a mom."

"What?" This time the shout came from several voices.

"Neither you nor I saw one single female the whole time we were on Xhroll. Their females are mothers only and don't do other types of work or go strolling about for you to see them. When did you ever see an abba?"

"But . . . but the abbas . . . they . . . they aren't . . . "

"They are. They're the same thing you are to them. Mothers. Breeders. Females. All the others are males."

When she turned to leave, the only sound that could be heard was that of Nico vomiting.

"Oh!" she added, turning back toward the group, ready to launch the rest of the lie. "And they can impregnate our men, as you well know. Not our women. Nor can our men impregnate their males, no matter how female they look. Also, thanks to the hero in our midst, Lieutenant Nico Andrade, the Xhroll have now learned that it's possible to impregnate a male whether he wants it or not, that it's possible to rape. It hadn't ever occurred to them before, poor third-worlders."

She looked back from the doorway and was content to see that Nico wasn't the only one throwing up.

Commander Kaminsky, who was talking with the Catholic chaplain, caught Charlie gently by the elbow as she was heading down the corridor that led to her cubicle.

"Captain, I don't want to hold you up, you deserve a few hours of rest, but the Xhroll have asked me to find you, discreetly. They would like to say goodbye."

Charlie turned around and began walking in the opposite direction, flanked by Kaminsky and the chaplain.

"Fonseca, a question, off the record. Sheer curiosity. Is it really true that those Xhroll don't have anything at all of interest to us?"

"Yes, it's true, commander. Unless you value landscaping manuals. You've already seen that the Xhroll ships are nothing to envy when compared to the Fleet's. And the Xhroll don't even have extraplanetary stations or bases."

"Weapons?"

"My personal opinion is that they have something they're saving for extreme cases but don't want to display or use. I could be wrong of course, sir."

"What about mining?"

"Nothing that we don't have. It's all in the report."

"Couldn't we at least send them a few missionary priests?" the chaplain interjected.

Charlie suppressed a smile.

"I suppose you could, Father. They're polite people. They would give them a nice welcome."

"But is there any chance of converting them? What do you think? They love life and Nature, isn't that right? They love the work of the divine. From there to believing in God is but a step. Tell me, Captain Fonseca, do you think it's possible?"

Charlie and Kaminsky exchanged a look.

"Not very, Father, to be honest. The Xhroll aren't very interested in future contact with us. They said so a thousand times."

"Well, you never know. I'll get in touch with the Holy Father," he concluded, rubbing his hands.

Hithrolgh and Ankhjaia'langtxhrl were waiting for Charlie at the entrance to their ship in hangar number three. She looked at them from afar for a second as if it were the first and not the last time: tall, slender, inscrutable, dressed from head to toe in black with an open-necked, sleeveless white tunic worn as a concession to their hosts' tastes. Alien. Distant. Cold. And yet filled with a love almost incomprehensible to humans, a global, pluralistic, abstract love.

Ankkhaia smiled when he saw Charlie. It was coming along; it almost looked like a smile now. Hithrolgh tried to copy it, without success.

"Is the hol'la alright?" was the first question.

"As right as rain. I've agreed to be its legal guardian."

"You are its abba's ari-arkhj. It is your right."

"Yes. Nico has renounced all claims."

"Is there any reason to be worried about his behavior?" Ankkhaia asked.

"Not anymore. I've wounded his pride and deflated his ego, in public. I don't think he'll cause any problems." She felt no scruples about neglecting to mention that she'd had to spread a few lies or, well, inaccuracies. "In a few hours everyone will be talking about how he taught the Xhroll how to rape human males. I don't think anyone will bother you in future."

"Now we have a future, Troschwkjai. Thanks to you."

"What's that name you called me?"

"Your new Xhroll name. It means 'one who forges a new path to a beautiful place without harming the natural life around it.'"

"That's a beautiful name."

Ankhjaia'langtxhrl looked at Hithrolgh with an unfamiliar expression on his enigmatic face. Then, turning to Charlie:

"Troschwkjai, within seven of our months, when the hol'la I implanted in Hithrolgh is born, we would like you to choose its name."

"I will. If you send me an official invitation and come get me, I'll travel to Xhroll with the hol'la so that it can start getting to know its other planet."

"What are you going to name it?"

Charlie smiled.

"First I'll have to figure out what sex it is. We humans think that's important right from the start. For now, I'm calling her Lenny."

Charlie was tempted to hug Ankkhaia goodbye. After all they were friends. But she remembered in time that two ari-arkhjs do not share physical contact. Nor was touch permitted with a xhrea, but Hithrolgh was an abba now. Since Charlie had never known an abba, she didn't know if an ari-arkhj would be allowed contact, so she merely crossed her arms over her chest.

"See you later, friends," was all she could think to say.

Ankhjaia'langtxhrl turned and entered the ship. Hithrolgh drew closer to Charlie.

"Could you get me information about the legal evolution of your species' abba? I know it would be more appropriate to ask an abba for this information, but I do not have relations with any other xhri and I do not have a lot of time."

Charlie couldn't believe her ears.

"What for? There's nothing in common."

"Now there is. I have been xhrea my entire life. I am a physician and a member of one of the circles that make policy concerning contact with xhris. Upon becoming an abba I must change my personal legal status, but that seems unacceptable to me. My case is not unique. Many xhrea will become abba when we have proven that the ari-arkhj can implant in us when we have reached maturity. The Xhroll social structure is going to undergo major changes. We may obtain thousands of new lives, but the xhrea, as xhrea, will be threatened. We must be prepared. We need your experience."

Ankhjaia'langtxhrl reappeared.

"Hithrolgh, I apologize for my conduct. I have not gotten used to the idea that you are an abba now and I cannot leave you alone without a voice to speak for you."

Hithrolgh looked at Charlie and, for the first time since that now long-ago first contact with the Xhroll, she saw an expression in his eyes. Mockery? Annoyance? Complicity?

Sisterly solidarity?

Charlie laughed at the foolish notion. That was totally impossible. For Hithrolgh, for Ankkhaia, for all of Xhroll, Charlie was one of her species' ari-arkhjs, a male xhri. It was an error that would have to be corrected sooner or later, but not now. Not yet.

Hithrolgh settled into the floating chair and together with Ankkhaia slowly disappeared into the ship's interior. Charlie glanced at her watch and took off running toward sickbay. Lenny had become the *Victoria*'s official mascot. Surely, someone would have started feeding her her bottle, but Charlie wanted to do it herself. After all, Lenny was her daughter.

Or her son.

And she was her mother.

Or her father.

Or his mother.

Or his father. Or . . .

She stopped running and, still at a brisk pace, began to whistle.

CPSIA information can be obtained
at www.ICGtesting.com
Printed in the USA
LVHW030039131121
703236LV00016B/1562

9 780826 502339